T0115208

Esther and the Bloodwood Flute

Esther and the Bloodwood Flute

VOL. 2 THE BLOODWOOD FLUTE SERIES

Lurlynn L. Potter

ISBN: Softcover 978-1-6641-7393-4
eBook 978-1-6641-7392-7

Print information available on the last page.

Rev. date: 05/10/2021

To order additional copies of this book, contact:
Xlibris
844-714-8691
www.Xlibris.com
Orders@Xlibris.com
827393

Contents

Chapter I

SAN FRANCISCO

She saw her reflection in the mirror, but something was not quite right. Her long flowing auburn hair flowed in gentle curves over her shoulders. A single streak of blonde softly made its way from her left temple in a wave of its own. Her Russet-colored eyes almost matched her hair, except for that pie-wedged section of gold in her left eye. It wasn't exactly a mirror she was looking at; it was more like water.

Esther reached her hand out to touch her reflection, but stopped just short of making contact. *"What is there to be afraid of?"* she chided herself as she reached forward again. As her hand began to make contact there was a slight resistance, then her arm was drawn through her reflection, immediately pulling her entire body with it!

The disorientation only lasted a moment, and the sensation of swirling lights and stars slowly dissipated as Esther gradually sat up, took a deep breath, and surveyed her surroundings. She was sitting near a river in a beautiful country scene with rolling emerald hills in the distance. It was late springtime, the air was heavily moist, and the foliage was deeply green. She could almost *smell* the green. The sun was hot, and despite the moisture in the air, the pathway near her raised a choking thick cloud of dust as horses rushed past her.

She stood up and saw thousands of men, women, and children crowded near a riverbed waiting to board a ferry. Their clothing was like the American pioneers of the 1800's (long fabric skirts, men wearing fabric pants with suspenders, and boots with long boot straps that flapped as they walked), but some of them wore a mixture of deerskin and leather with fabric vests, shirts, and turban head-wraps or large-brimmed hats. They looked dejected and sorrowful as they waited with baskets, woven bags, and trunks. Uniformed men on horses surrounded the forlorn group, taunting them and laughing. Children were crying unconsolably.

Nearby, Esther could see a family being forced to leave their home at rifle point. The two-story red-brick home with two chimneys, white trim around the doors and windows, and white columns near the balcony and front porch was elegant. The neatly manicured bushes and shrubbery were indicative of tender care. The wooden shingles were in good repair; every evidence of prosperity.

Nevertheless, cherished belongings were being tossed out and broken as the enforcers were rummaging through the prized possessions that had been carefully packed. Occasionally, an item would be pocketed with a hoot. Eventually, the disconsolate family was allowed to join their fellow Cherokee brothers-in-waiting for another ferry boat to take them across the Tennessee River as a first step in the long journey to their new lands. There was no hint of resistance from the proud race, only sorrowful compliance and tears. Lots of tears.

In the distance, she could hear a woman somewhere desperately and franticly screaming and crying in a panicked way for someone to help her. Men were laughing. Eventually the screaming was muffled, then stopped altogether. Esther could only imagine what was happening somewhere in the alleyway nearby, and it horrified her.

A home, made of logs and bricks, was lit on fire by men on horses who were hooting and hollering as the belongings of the dejected were exploding in flames and disappearing as black billowing clouds of smoke consumed them.

It had only been a momentary flash, but Esther could hardly bear it. She turned away from the awful scene and peered into the nearby stream.

Her reflection was familiar but distorted. She reached out to touch her image, but was instantly pulled back into the tide.

Esther sat up in bed, breathless. It had been a dream! But it seemed so real… well, almost real.

She threw on some sweats and a T-shirt, yawned and went downstairs to grab a bite to eat. She wasn't actually hungry, but needed to do something to shake off the melancholy mood that was threatening to overtake her. Michael was hunched over a bowl of cereal reading the latest news on an iPad. He was totally oblivious to the entrance of his daughter as she plopped down across the table from him while simultaneously peeling a banana.

Without moving he mumbled, "Sleep well?" "Like a log," she lied. Esther studied her father. His dark wavy hair just covered the top of his ears and hit the edge of his collar. His brows were bushy and furrowed as he studied the screen before him, his chocolate eyes squinting at the small print. He sensed his daughter staring at him, and raising his eyebrows, revealing a deeply creviced forehead.

"What?" he asked edgily.

Esther studied his features. Although he was only 45, he looked weary and old. Yet, there was a rugged handsomeness to her father. The stubble on his face was visible, even though he had obviously shaved that morning. She tried to imagine him young and vibrant like when he met her mother, Ziven, in Jerusalem. She tried to imagine what her mother saw in him then that drew them together.

She rehearsed the story in her mind – not that her father had given her many details – she had read most of it in her mother's journal. According to her mother, her father had been helping someone replace shingles on their roof, and was behaving carelessly. He was probably trying to impress young Ziven as she passed by. Then, he fell 30 feet in slow motion right in front of her mother and had made a dreadful noise while hitting the concrete. Ziven was frightened and ran to Michael's side. She was tending to him when he opened his eyes, blinked a few times, then smiled and just stared at her with a dazed look on his face. Michael had told Esther that this was the moment he fell in love with her mother. That was the moment he knew he would marry her someday.

"Nothing," she lied again as she stood and spun on her heel. She had a busy day today and didn't have time to get into another discussion. Every discussion seemed to evolve into an interrogation with endless questions. She loved her father, but he didn't understand her, and she didn't have patience for him right now. Besides, this week was finals week, and she needed to clear her mind and catch the BART. Her finals were at University of San Francisco. If all went well, she would graduate this week with a double major: a Master of Professional Science in Biotechnology and a Master of Science in Microbiology.

Esther was only 22 years old, but she graduated from high school a year early with 20 AP college credit hours which gave her a head start at college. Besides, math and science had always come easily to her, they just made sense.

Esther had always felt as though she were cheating because she could see between the molecules of solid objects, could feel their energy, and sense their various momentums. Plant and animal life were easy to communicate with, and this seemed to give her an edge above her college colleagues as well. She knew she was different, and she liked it that way, but sometimes she did feel a bit lonely and isolated. She realized that she should take responsibility for her part in her emotional and social seclusion. Someday when she had less on her plate, she would spend the necessary time to analyze what exactly that meant. *"I'll think about that tomorrow… I sound like Scarlet O'Hara in Gone with the Wind!"* she thought to herself with a smirk, shaking her head.

Chapter II

THE BOW

"Open it!" Michael said bouncing as excitedly like a young boy on Christmas morning. It was Esther's 23rd birthday, and she had plans with friends. However, her father had convinced her to spend the day with him instead. Reluctantly she had agreed and was trying to hide her lack of enthusiasm. She knew he meant well, and after all, he was her father.

She looked at his wide smile of anticipation as he brought a package from behind his back and set it on the table. She chuckled and shook her head at the package that didn't even try to disguise its contents with another shape. It was obviously a bow and arrow set.

"Let me guess… It's a sweater!" she raised one eyebrow and teased him with a cock of her head.

She ripped open the pink wrapping paper with butterflies and flowers (the same wrapping paper used to conceal every birthday gift she ever received from her father over the past 23 years) to reveal a 62-inch Samick Sage Takedown Recurve Bow. It was elegant and beautiful. Along with it were a dozen hand-carved wooden arrows with four narrow stripes near the end: yellow, red, white, and black. These four colors together represent "balance" because they signify the four directions to the Cherokee. She had read that in a book.

Esther looked up to see her father eagerly watching her hands gently inspected the arrows he had made for her as she fought the urge to snatch up the bow. Her hands gently moved along the smooth lines of the arrows, then she watched them roll back and forth in her fingers. They were perfectly straight. The wood was strong, smooth, and heavy. "What kind of wood is this?" she queried. "Ash" he replied. "It had a mind of its own, but I got them straightened out alright."

"*Yes, it does have a mind of its own,*" she thought to herself. She could see lightning flashes of memory the arrows were sharing with her about their former life as a large Ash tree giving shade, providing shelter to birds and insects, and adding beauty to the lawn of a park near a children's playground long ago. A larger building was being built, so the beautiful Ash tree had been cut down, sliced, and shipped to a wear-house where Michael had found and purchased one piece of the great one. "*What is my purpose now?*" it spoke to her. Esther was careful not to react with her father watching her so closely. "*You will only be used to do good,*" she promised the arrows as she respectfully set them down on the kitchen table.

Next, she picked up the fiberglass bow and turned it to see the curves of every angle. Her eyes were squinted as she studied its features and then pulled back the 40-pound string, pretending to aim at the refrigerator handle, and let the imaginary arrow fly. "It's beautiful, Aba!" she gushed as she rushed into her father's arms. "Thank you!"

"Aba" is the Hebrew word for "father" that represents an intimate closeness like "daddy" in English. Her father was an Israeli citizen with a green card to work in the United States. He didn't speak much of the old country or life before he came to America. He usually fought to hold back the tears when he did, so naturally, he avoided the subject altogether.

Esther's mother, Ziven, had been raised in Jerusalem, but was born Cherokee. She had been adopted by her grandparents who were killed in an explosion there before Esther was born. Then, there was a sister born in America that died just before her birth. Esther had seen the marker in the grave next to her mother's grave at the old cemetery by the North Beach Chabad Synagogue on Lombard Street near Fisherman's Wharf. Batia's gravestone said, "Our Beloved Firstborn – Returned to God."

And, her mother's gravestone said, "Heaven is now brighter, Earth is left in darkness."

Esther's father startled her, bringing her back to the present, as he suddenly exploded with the rest of the surprise and the words spilled out all at once, sort of like an explosion. "I thought we could go practice with your new bow. There is an outdoor target range not far from here that will teach you how to use it and give you experience in estimating distances so you know which mark to use when aiming. There's even a special booklet here that gives you all of the instructions for your new bow." Esther just shook her head and smiled to herself while thinking, *"He is my father!"*

Before she knew it, she and her father were getting off of the BART and walking toward a remote hill southeast of San Francisco. She shot off a couple of arrows when she was startled by a woman's scream. The slender woman had dark shoulder-length medium brown hair. Two men had her by the arms and were forcing her into a white van with no windows. One of the men had his hand over her mouth. She was wearing black pants, a loose pull-over, and flats for shoes. Her legs were flailing and trying to trip up her assailants. Her body was unsuccessfully writhing and twisting to get away. The men were struggling to get control and threw her into the open compartment. One man jumped into the van and slid the side door closed while the other man hopped into the passenger side of the van, shut the door, and gave the motion to take off.

In that split second, Esther had selected an arrow, placed it between the first and second fingers of her left hand, pulled the string back with her right hand, and had begun making her calculations.

"Let's see, if this bow is rated at a velocity of 300 feet per second, and a flying arrow will accelerate towards earth at about 30 feet per second… and it will fall around 75 inches per 0.2 seconds, or 200 inches per second… that's about 16.5 feet per second… and that van is about 600 yards away, that's about 1,800 feet… and it is probably going 30 miles per hour or 44 feet per second… then I'll probably have to give it about a 50 foot lead and aim about 20 feet high…

"Ash tree arrow, fly straight and true, and you will do some good today," she thought silently as she pulled the string back—touching her lip for stability – took a breath, and then gently let her arrow fly.

It seemed as though the wooden arrow were flying in slow motion. There was no wind, yet it seemed to be caught in a current that lifted it upward in a delicate arch. As it began to descend, the arrow seemed to speed up as it fixated on its target like a missile.

Suddenly there was a large popping sound as the arrow hit the right front wheel of the escaping van, sending it into a sideways skid and directly into a concrete barrier. In a moment's notice, the van was surrounded by officials in black suits with badges and Glock 19 handguns, all pointed at the perpetrators and shouting for everyone to come out with their hands up.

Michael's jaw dropped as he gaped at his daughter. She never did cease to amaze him! She was so much like her mother! He looked at his grown-up daughter with a new respect and admiration.

For a moment, Michael let his mind drift to a time, not so long ago, when his beloved Ziven was alive. For a brief moment, he compared the features of these two amazing women: Ziven's eyes were hazel and sometimes golden. They had a dark circle of deep green around the perimeter of her irises. He had been mesmerized by her eyes the first day he met her. With her light brown hair, and olive complexion, she was a true beauty.

Esther's eyes didn't have that dark circle around the irises, but they were truly unique. They used to be hazel when she was young, but changed as she became a teenager. Now, as an adult, her eyes were a rusty color that looked magical with her auburn hair. In fact, they were almost the same color as her hair, except for a golden pie-wedge shaped section in the lower part of her left eye. It was as though shiny gold was hidden away inside his daughter that just had to make itself known somewhere. It was intriguing and seemed to draw a person in before they even realized they were staring.

Esther's nose was not as large as Ziven's. It was more delicate. Her lips were fuller, and her cheek bones were not as high. She was also taller than her mother had been, but her other features seemed far more delicate all around.

And sometime shortly after her dark baby hair had rubbed off, Esther's hair became the most beautiful color of auburn Michael had ever seen. That was, except for a little strip of blonde that grew naturally near her left ear. It was a magical effect that made anyone who met his daughter instantly fall in love with her.

Ziven would have been so proud at this moment. He imagined how she would feel if she were alive today and could see the strong, beautiful daughter Esther had become. He knew he felt proud.

Being back in the moment, the father and daughter looked at each other. Michael's broad smile turned into a childish giggle. Esther giggled too. After all, what she had just done was fun!

Chapter III

TWO MEN IN TRENCH COATS

Esther sat at the kitchen table with papers scattered all around and in various piles, her laptop nearby, deeply concentrating and focused on the task at hand. She had graduated *magna cum laude* with a double major: a Master of Professional Science in Biotechnology and a Master of Science in Microbiology at one of the most prestigious universities in the nation – University of San Francisco. Before she knew it, she was being solicited by large corporations to visit their companies and to consider interviewing with them. Now she needed to do her own research to decide which companies to visit, and which to send "no, thank you" reply letters to.

She had narrowed it down to a microbiologist position at Centers for Disease Control and Prevention in Atlanta, Georgia; Public Health Microbiologist for San Diego County, California; and was looking at a position as a Medical Technologist in Washington, D.C. when her thoughts were interrupted by a loud knocking at the front door.

"We have a door bell," she muttered to herself sarcastically as she got up to answer the door.

There, standing before her, like something out of a cheesy spy movie, were two men wearing hats, sunglasses, and full-length trench coats. They looked so ridiculous that Esther had to stop herself from laughing out loud. She literally had to bite her lip. They were looking around the neighborhood from the corners of their eyes, trying not to look obvious.

As soon as she got control of herself, Esther managed to ask, "May I help you?" Her eyebrows were scrunched with one raised, and her eyes narrowed into a suspicious squint.

The shorter of the two stepped forward, raised his index finger and said, "That's exactly what we were hoping you would say!"

"Yup, these two are right out of a bad movie!" she thought to herself.

The taller, more slender man, gently pulled his friend back by the elbow and began to remove his sunglasses to reveal penetrating light blue eyes with long dark lashes and thick dark eye brows. He smiled, revealing a straight row of white teeth and a slight dimple in his left cheek. Then, after looking to his right and his left, and retrieving his identification from his side coat pocket, he asked, "Good morning Miss Cohan. We are with the USFDA. May we please come in? We have something of a most urgent nature to discuss with you."

Esther's father was at work, and she was not comfortable even letting repairmen come into the house when she was alone. She sized them up for a moment. Besides looking ridiculous in those costumes, these two reminded her of comedy teams she had seen in old black and white movies. Surely, there was nothing to fear with these two.

Suddenly, she noticed something more. As she looked at the center of the form of the shorter man, her peripheral vision could sense his energy field. It was like heat rising off hot pavement in the summertime, bending the images in the background as it did. The area around Thomas Jepson was solid and thick. Then, she began to see his aura. It was creamy white, solid and thick as well.

She glanced over at the taller man. Robert Beecham was staring at her with amusement now. This made her feel uncomfortable, but she needed to be sure she could trust them before inviting these two strangers into her home.

She looked down from his eyes so she wouldn't be distracted. As she stared at his chest, she could then see his aura too. Her eyes carefully followed the outline of his frame to see radiating light surrounding him. This light was brighter than that of his partner's. It seemed to stream far beyond his physical body with rays of brightness extending that made her feel totally at ease.

"You may come in," she finally said. Esther ushered the two strangers into the living room and gestured for them to sit on the sofa. "May I offer you something to drink?" "No, thank you," they said in unison as they removed their hats and sat down. Thomas finally removed his sunglasses and began scanning the room, but Robert kept his eyes on Esther.

There was a moment of awkward silence before they each began to speak at once. They chuckled, then Esther asked, "What is it you want to discuss that is so important?"

Robert sat forward, "We know that you have received several letters of interest from microbiology companies. Have you made up your mind about any of them yet?"

Esther spied him suspiciously, "How did you know that?"

Thomas interrupted quickly, "Well, of course you would have received letters. You just graduated at the top of your class!"

Esther began to regret inviting these strangers into her home. They knew far too much about her and she knew nothing about them. She was feeling somewhat exposed and vulnerable. "What government agency did you say you were with, and may I please see your identification again?" she politely asked. They handed over their wallets. "*United States Food and Drug Administration*" it said. "*Special Ops—hmm I wonder what that means.*"

Both wallets were well worn. Neither seemed to have much cash in them but they were bulging with cards and receipts. Esther decided to answer their questions and returned their wallets to them.

As she handed over the wallets, there was a moment when their hands were touching their wallets at the same time. In a flash, Esther could see the last 24 hours of their lives. She viewed their relationship, their heart-to-heart discussions as they waited for her father to leave, and she sensed the strong familial ties the taller one had with his family. He had a peace that emanated from being grounded in a profound faith. She sensed that this helped him deal with the fear of danger from his job and gave him a sense of purpose in all areas of his life. He seemed to have great patriotism as well. She also sensed that the shorter of the two was a musician and also a good man who deeply respected his partner.

"I was actually just going through my options when you came to the door," she answered, trying not to stammer.

Robert stood up, gently touched her arm, looked into her eyes and softly said, "Please be sure to consider the position with the Department of Forensic Sciences in Washington, D.C. Its location will make things much easier."

Esther gave him a questioning look. Thomas stood up and said, "We will be in contact with you later. Have a nice day." And just like that, they were gone.

Esther shook her head, sighed, and returned to the kitchen and to the task of contacting the companies she was interested in; but she couldn't get the image of Robert's aura out of her mind. She hadn't seen anything like that before. And, his eyes. They seemed to have etched themselves into her mind like a faint after-image. So much so, that she could see them when she closed her eyes many moments later.

Chapter IV

SAN DIEGO

Esther had an appointment to meet with the HR Director of San Diego County for the Public Health Microbiologist position open there. She had decided to take a drive in her new car along the coast and see some of the sights along the way. She had saved up and paid cash for her 2013 cream VW Beetle convertible. It only had 23,000 miles on it and was worth much more than the $16,000 she paid for it.

Driving her "bug" gave her a feeling of freedom and satisfaction she had never felt before. As she sat in the light leather seats, she sensed the life-force remaining in them. Even the molecules from the car's metal, glass, fiberglass, and rubber tires emitted a continual pulsing praise to The Creator. She could feel it move through her as she drove down California Interstate-1. Even though it would add a couple of extra hours to her trip, she opted not to take Interstate-5 so she could drive along the beautiful coastline.

When she reached Point Montara, she stopped to walk around and get a better look at the white lighthouse on a cliff overlooking the ocean.

It was solid and beautiful. She imagined ships coming in and the light of this lighthouse cutting through the dense fog warning them, guiding them, saving them.

As Esther imagined what this must have been like for so many people of the past, she heard, "*Such inspiration is not only a thing of the past. You are a lighthouse today. Just let your light shine.*" It's not that she actually "heard" it, it's more like she "felt" it. She took a deep breath and expanded her senses. She could feel the molecules of the stone she was sitting on; their motion and obedience to law. She could feel its energy and life force moving through her.

The sensation flowed from her like a tremendous wave of light, illuminating all life around her. She was able to differentiate life below the surface, life in the air, and life into the water far past the horizon. She closed her eyes for a moment, took another deep breath and paid attention to a school of fish near the reef, then watched a ray floating on the waves, and then caught sight of a family of dolphins. She felt them communicate that it was time to "play" as they headed toward the surface of the water.

Esther opened her eyes and laughed in delight as she saw these dolphins crest the ocean surface, leap high above it, and splash happily again and again. The next few moments were spent in expressions of gratitude to The Creator for allowing her to feel these things and to be so connected with nature in a way that seemed so "un-natural" to so many others. It was such a part of who she was. A part that has always given her great fulfillment, yet has also made her feel somewhat lonely at the same time, for there was no one she could share these thoughts and feelings with. For some reason, she had trouble trusting this part of herself with anyone… not even with her father. How Esther missed her mother! She never knew her, but yet missed her terribly!

Shrugging off melancholy feelings that threatened to envelop her, Esther hopped into her car and drove a few more miles, enjoying the beautiful vistas until she stopped at San Luis Obisbo to stretch her legs and get some gas. She decided to leave her parked car and walk a couple of blocks to the beach to see if she could get something to eat there. Her appointment with Marie Florence, HR Director at San Diego County wasn't until the next morning, so she had plenty of time.

Esther removed her taupe scrunchie and let the salty ocean breeze blow her hair behind her as she walked toward the ocean. This time she took her mother's Bloodwood Flute with her in a deerskin case. She didn't know if she would be playing it, but she always brought it with her in case she had an opportunity like this. It was perfect.

The white sand was cool, deep, and loose as she walked closer to the shore. Eventually, the color darkened, and the moist sand became firm and unyielding. Esther could see the lighthouse at Pigeon Point in the distance to the north. To the south, she could hear laughter around a barrel that had some flames in it and shadows of a group of young people surrounding it.

The sound of waves crashing along the shoreline was almost deafening yet had a soothing, healing effect on her. She found an old log that had washed up on the shore long ago, and sat on it. She had long since removed her shoes, and set them down on the sand next to her purse. She watched seagulls glide on the breeze with their heads down, looking for a fish to swim near enough to the surface so they could dive down and snag a bite for dinner.

As Esther kept her eyes on the horizon, where the living water touches the sky, she could feel the rotation of the earth beneath her. It's slow and steady roll away from the sun made her feel secure and confident that all things are part of one great whole. She felt sure that Someone or Something was Architect of all of this beauty and the delicate balance that is Nature.

Chapter V

THE BLOODWOOD FLUTE

Esther pulled out her mother's Bloodwood Flute. She hadn't played it for a while. It's not that she didn't like to play it; the melodies and tones it made were so beautiful and warm. It's that it was more than just a flute to her, and required privacy.

Each time she began to play it, Esther would be pulled into another place and time. Her mother, Ziven, would be there, and she would have long conversations with her. She would give Esther confidence, advice, and profound insight. Esther treasured those moments, life just seemed to get busy sometimes.

Esther had never shared this secret with her father. He didn't seem to understand her other special gifts when she had tried to share them with him, so this was definitely one to keep to herself.

The ocean breeze was refreshing and cool. The brilliant fiery orb was low in the sky and would be setting soon. Esther put the flute to her mouth and gently began to blow. She never planned what to play. The flute just seemed to be in charge of that. The melody that flowed from the flute this time was haunting and smooth.

Instantly, she found herself in a mountain scene somewhere. There was a waterfall nearby and a beautiful lake. The trees were green, and some had blossoms. Wild flowers were everywhere, and fresh floral scents were lilting on the air.

Barely aware of her true surroundings as she continued to play the Native American flute; her mother, Ziven, stood before her. "Darling, are you nervous, or excited?"

"A little of both, I guess." Esther answered. "How will I know which is the best decision to make?"

"When you come to a fork in the road, you must let your heart guide you. It always will, as long as you listen to it," her mother answered, then instantly faded away.

Suddenly, Esther found herself alone on the beach. She stood up and made her way to the seashore, leaving her shoes behind. As she stepped into the receding wave, she could feel the cool wet sand dissolve below her weight. She wriggled her toes as the next wave advanced and covered her feet with surprisingly warm bubbles. The water near San Francisco was quite a bit cooler, so she very much enjoyed this surprise.

The salty air was as soothing as a sleepy summers' evening. The sun began to set and the sky turned fire-orange. The reflection of the sunset on the foam and the withdrawing water was doubly beautiful. As Esther continued to play the Bloodwood Flute, the sun finally set and she felt her heart calm within her.

With each pulsing wave, Esther felt a connection grow with all living creatures in the ocean; the blue whale, dolphin, angel fish, starfish, and krill. She became part of their joys and their sorrows. She felt their fears and their triumphs; she was "one" with them all. Their consciousness was her consciousness. The surreal feeling welled up inside of her until it consumed her entire being.

Esther played the flute again as she felt these feelings, this fusion of energy and light, combined with the beautiful shimmering music the water was contributing to the sound of the Bloodwood Flute, generated a symphonic ecstasy. She felt the urge to praise God! She felt the urge to sing within her soul a song of praise to The Creator of all things. It was an overwhelming distillation of pure delight!

The Bloodwood Flute sang its own song. *"I sing praise! The daughter of my Ziven feels the joy of oneness when she plays me. I sing praise that I am alive! I sing honor, praise, glory, and joy to The Creator of all things!"*

Chapter VI

INTERVIEWS

Marie Florence sat behind a large mahogany desk looking at a computer screen when Esther was ushered in. Marie was dressed in a dark pin-striped business suit that seemed too large for her, a red silk buttoned shirt, pencil skirt, and red pumps. Her dark hair was pulled back into a pony tail, and her lipstick was distractingly bright red.

"Hello, I am Marie Florence. You must be Esther Cohan," she said as she reached out her hand. Esther experienced the familiar flash of the last 24 hours of Marie's life.

Marie was a middle-aged woman who was going through a divorce. She had lost a lot of weight, hadn't slept in weeks, and poured herself into her work to avoid the stark reality of her mundane life. Just before Esther had entered the room, Marie had been on the phone with her lawyer who informed her that her husband was seen with another woman at a local hotel.

Marie didn't have time to assimilate this news yet. She just felt sort of numb, and pressed on – knowing that she would probably cry herself to sleep later.

"Have a seat," Marie said as she gestured to a leather upholstered chair. As Esther looked around Ms. Florence's office, she could see a few themes: butterflies and music. Esther took the opportunity to tell her interviewer about the Bloodwood Flute her mother had made, and that she likes to play it whenever she can. This seemed to warm up their discussion. Esther wanted to find a way to make this woman's day a little better.

"I noticed that you also like butterflies," Esther contributed.

"Oh yes!" Marie gushed. "My favorite is the Tiger Swallow-tail!"

"Mine too!" Esther hesitated, deciding whether to share the next experience or not. Upon seeing Ms. Florence lean forward in anticipation of an explanation, she decided to continue.

Esther began. "Once, in late spring, I noticed a paper-thin cocoon attached to the steps in front of our house. I watched with fascination as a beautiful Tiger Swallow-tail butterfly emerged from within. Its long black legs came out first and I saw it strain to pull the colorful wings behind it. I let it climb upon my hand and watched as it pumped its heavy wet wings with great effort over and over again until they were finally light and dry. At the moment the butterfly flew away, I sensed the release of joy that it felt at that instant. It was a beautiful experience!"

Marie was breathless as she imagined that moment. There was silence for a while as they both absorbed the beauty and majesty of the memory that had been shared.

Before she knew it, Marie Florence had offered her the job. "May I have a couple of days to consider it? I have a couple of other interviews I'd like to complete before I make up my mind," Esther answered in a daze.

"Of course," Marie replied. "We'll be in touch next week."

Esther returned home enjoying the ride and feeling quite pleased at having an option for her future. She remembered what her mother had said and tried to listen to her heart, when a song suddenly came to her mind. She'd never heard it before. It was a sweet simple melody; calming and peaceful. She would have to remember it and try to play it on the Bloodwood Flute later. It stayed with her until she reached her home and collapsed in her own bed for the night.

The flight to Atlanta was uneventful. Esther was not nervous, but she didn't know what to expect. All she knew is that it would be colder and more humid there than in San Francisco. As she flew over Georgia, she was surprised to see so many trees. It seemed that there was not a single area of bare ground anywhere. *"Beautiful!"* she silently exclaimed.

A man in a dark polyester suit was holding a sign that said, "COHAN" when she got off the plane. He carried her luggage to the car and drove her to the hotel, making no effort to engage in small talk—which was just fine with her. The four-hour time difference had left her feeling a bit tired anyway.

Every freeway was lined with large trees including: Ash, Maple, and Cedar. Even if the freeway was high in the air, these behemoths on all sides were towering over the edges. Many trees had long lacy Spanish Moss hanging from their branches. "*There must be lots of moisture in the air all year long*," she thought to herself.

Next to several freeways, were ponds that had fences around their perimeters. When she questioned the driver about this, he simply said, "Alligators." She found herself looking more intently perchance she might see one. She had only seen alligators and crocodiles in the zoo, and was fascinated with them. They have many physical similarities, but genetically, they split into separate genera too long ago to be actually related. Nevertheless, seeing an alligator in Georgia, most likely meant that someone brought a cute little pet home, and released it later. This is the case with most alligators in the region.

Before reaching the hotel, they passed a cemetery. Esther was surprised to see it full of small mausoleums. She supposed it was because the water table is so high there, it makes more sense to care for deceased loved ones that way. It also made for a decoratively beautiful cemetery… as cemeteries go.

She had two hours to rest before her interview with the HR Director of Centers for Disease Control and Prevention, so Esther decided to go for a short walk. The air was moist and chill, but there was no breeze. Next to the sidewalk was dense foliage. Esther could sense the life force of the trees as they reached higher and higher for any amount of sunlight they could grasp. She could feel them breath in the moisture with the air and sensed the tingling energy that this gave them all the way to the depths of their root tips.

At the same time, however, she sensed something else. Something was not right. She needed to return to the hotel. NOW!

She had learned to follow her impressions without second-guessing the reasons why. So, she didn't see the man at the next intersection who had been talking on his phone… and waiting for her.

Alan Davidson was at the end of his career. Only six more months to go before he could retire. He had been instrumental in selecting several employees who had made tremendous contributions to public health and averted some disastrous pandemics the public was not even aware of. He was very proud to be part of such a prestigious company, and he felt very protective of that reputation.

As Esther Cohan walked into his office, he was surprised at how young she was. He glanced at her resume again and estimated that she should be at least 30 years old, but she was obviously much younger than that.

His years of experience in Human Resources told him that he could not let her age be a factor of any kind in making such decisions, so he summarily dismissed those thoughts from his mind. He stood, smiled, and extended his hand. Her confidence was evident in the way she swiftly reached for his hand and gave it a firm shake.

As Esther took Alan's hand, the flashes from the last 24 hours of his. life were very distracting to her. This man struggled to stay focused. No one knew he suffered from severe depression. He hid it well, even from his family. Somehow, over the years he found tricks to disguise his anguish from everyone around him. Something made him keep going when his world seemed to be hopelessly dismal. It was his love for his family. Whenever he wanted to end it all, he thought of what that would do to his family, and he was somehow able to claw his way out of the deep pit of despair he often found himself in.

As she looked into his eyes, she saw his aura. It was not smooth, it was "ribbed" and had tints of green at the edges. Gaining her composure, and feeling overwhelmed with compassion for this man, she slowly sat down.

Esther was wearing a conservative moss-green suit with a ruffled rust-colored shirt that complimented her flowing auburn hair beautifully. She was extremely beautiful – even captivating, but he was a professional and could not let that distract him, nor persuade him in any way.

The standard interview questions were answered with precision and impressive competence. She didn't seem to show any signs of nervousness or hesitancy as she answered even the most difficult of questions.

Her quick wit and confidence also won over Alan's colleagues in subsequent interviews, and before he knew it, he had offered her the job and they were negotiating the details. Esther left with another offer on the table to consider, and a big smile on her face.

Chapter VII

WASHINGTON, D.C.

Esther took a flight directly from Atlanta to Washington, D.C. for her final interview. Once the plane was on the runway, there was a delay due to volatile weather, so they sat in their seats an additional 45 minutes before taking off.

During that time, she made a mental list of all the things she would need to do once this final interview was over, and she was back home. Obviously, she would be moving, and there were loose ends to tie up there, as well as all of the details about moving, such as: a change of address with the U.S. Postal Service, the DMV and registration for her car, finding an apartment, etc.

Eventually, the plane was ready and as it began speeding down the runway, the front wheel lifted off. Suddenly the front of the plane fell with a crash and the aircraft screeched to a bouncing halt. Overhead compartments popped open and personal items fell onto the heads of frightened passengers sitting near the isles. People were screaming and holding on desperately to the seats in front of them as the plane threw everyone forward. Children were crying hysterically and unconsolably.

Esther realized that she had been holding her breath. Blinking her eyes a few times, and taking a deep breath, she suddenly jerked. "I… I'm so sorry!" she stammered. Then, blushing, she continued, "I didn't realize I had grabbed your hand!"

Massaging his newly released hand, Todd Bristol simply smiled and said, "That's quite alright. I wasn't planning to use it for a while anyway," he laughed heartily. Esther briefly glanced at the distinguished middle-aged man sitting next to her. He was clean shaven, had a slight dimple in his chin, wavy hair that lightly curled just at his collar, and a delightful British accent.

She suddenly realized that she hadn't seen the last 24 hours of this man's life when she touched him. Strange. Perhaps the anxiety of what was happening in the cabin distracted her. She didn't see it as suspicious, only an interesting puzzle.

Everyone inside the plane was strapped in for lift off, so no one was hurt, but those few moments of terror left everyone breathless and wide-eyed. Eventually, a muffled voice came over the loud speaker: "Uh… (clearing throat) please stay seated and remain calm! We'll give you more information as soon as we have it." Most passengers felt assured that they would be informed as to their status as soon as possible, but there always seems to be someone who is impatient and wants to know all the details immediately.

Not a word was spoken, but Esther slightly rolled her eyes, looked over at the distinguished gentleman sitting to her left, shook her head and thought, *"No comment!"* Todd Bristol chuckled.

Vehicles rushed to the side of the airplane while flight attendants unsuccessfully tried to calm and distract passengers with small bags of tiny pretzels and small cups filled with lots of ice and a little bit of juice or soft drink. Finally, the pilot announced that they had aborted their lift off because of a warning light on the flight panel. This resulted in the abrupt touchdown that caused a tire to pop. Both issues were now resolved, and the cabin crew was to prepare again – finally – for takeoff.

"Well, that was an adventure!" Todd smiled. Esther grinned and responded, "Indeed."

Esther breathed a sigh of relief when they were finally in the air. She was glad her interview was not until the next morning. She would need plenty of time to relax and prepare before meeting with Chloe Collins, the HR Director for the Department of Forensic Sciences. She closed her eyes to relax, and before she knew it, the plane was landing, and her new British friend was nowhere to be seen. *"Curious,"* she thought to herself after looking around. She hadn't had a chance to touch his arm to find out about him. "Oh well."

As before, a suited driver was waiting for her with a "COHAN" sign. He loaded her luggage and opened the door for Esther to get into the back seat. Esther felt something holding her back, as though she should not get into the car, but she shrugged the feeling off and got in anyway.

No sooner had the driver begun driving, but the doors locked and a dividing wall closed between the two of them, closing Esther inside with no way to get out. She frantically tried to open the windows and doors, and decided that since there was nothing she could do about it at this point, she would calm down and watch through the side windows to pay attention to where she was being taken. Then, at the first opportunity, she would make her escape. She had to keep her senses sharp and her mind clear.

She also fought the urge to chide herself for not listening to her feelings about not getting into the car in the first place. She wouldn't make that mistake again!

Eventually, the car stopped and the driver got out, but no one opened her door. She seemed to be inside a parking structure but had no idea where she was. The driver's side door suddenly opened, but she didn't see anyone. With no other option, she tentatively inched toward the opening to get a look around, her heart beating out of her chest, and her head pounding violently.

Senses heightened; she peeked through the slight opening to see two men in trench coats. They looked familiar… Thomas Jepson and Robert Beecham?! These were the two clowns that came to her home in San Francisco!

"You!" she exclaimed as Robert opened the door for her.

Thomas looked up at Robert who put his hands up apologetically and said, "Sorry if we startled you, Miss Cohan. We had to make sure you were not followed."

"What is going on?!" Esther demanded. Then, in a whisper and looking around she asked hesitantly, "Am I in danger?"

Thomas said, "Yes," at the same time Robert answered, "No."

"Do you two want to get your story straight and try that again?" she quipped (partially in earnest). Robert let Thomas take the lead. "Well, not exactly," he began. Then Thomas looked at Robert, who gave him the "go ahead" to continue.

"What we're about to tell you must not EVER be discussed with anyone else, ever! Not even your father. It would put that person in danger, and is a matter of national security. Do you understand?" He began intensely. Taken aback, Esther slowly answered, "I understand."

"You are half Cherokee, Native American, right?"

"Yes, my mother was Cherokee."

"There is a very serious threat to the Cherokee people that goes up to the highest ranks of the government." He handed her a thick manila envelope and said, "This file will give you more details. Please review it before your interview tomorrow with Ms. Collins."

"Why should I believe you?" Esther asked suspiciously.

"Because we're telling the truth!" Thomas volunteered quickly. Then he looked quickly at Robert for confirmation.

Robert began slowly. "In the early days of our nation when the Native Americans were exposed to Smallpox, those Cherokee who survived did so because they naturally had a special genetic anti-body. Over time, that anti-body has become stronger against certain diseases such as most cancer strains. The pharmaceutical companies that treat these cancers do not want anyone to find this out. They are systematically rounding up and killing every person with a Cherokee marker in their DNA so they can secretly exterminate all who might be able to help wipe out this disease or overturn their financial empire and power."

Robert stopped to assess Esther's reaction. She was a stone. *"I'd hate to play poker against her!"* he thought to himself.

"Many doctors across the nation order unnecessary blood tests for anyone they suspect has Cherokee heritage. They are trained to look for certain physical characteristics and slight mutations attributed to the Cherokee people. Most doctors don't know about this, however, so it's actually the labs that look for the DNA marker in every sample that comes through. (Most clinics send their lab work to only a few laboratories in the nation.)

"The next step is to prescribe medicine that would actually cause side effects that mimic the symptoms of the flu. When they take any cold medicine that has alcohol (or any alcohol for that matter) they die of a massive heart attack within hours in their sleep. This binary poisoning is impossible to detect in autopsies and doesn't show up in regular medical tests in the meantime either.

"We can't tell you any more right now, but we can say that if you choose to help us, the best place for us to easily communicate with you will be if you take the job with the Department of Forensic Sciences."

"I haven't even interviewed yet. What if they don't offer me the job?"

"They will." Robert continued, "It's not safe for us to meet with you face to face for a while. In that file," he said, gesturing toward the envelope in her hand, "you will find the methods for our future communications."

Thomas interjected, "You will need to destroy that file after you read it. Do you understand?"

Stunned, Esther responded, "Of course."

"Thank you," Robert said genuinely. Then, looking around quickly, said, "You need to get going, now. You can trust this driver."

Esther looked over at the man who picked her up from the airport. She could see his aura, and it was thin with ribbed layers. It wasn't very bright. Every instinct within her said that she could NOT trust him. She also decided that this moment was not the time to disclose her feelings. She would have to remain on the alert about this until she could talk to Robert and Thomas confidentially. Forcing a smile, she reluctantly agreed and nervously got back into the car.

Once they got going again, Esther tentatively reached her hand out to touch the seat behind the driver, hoping she could get a sense of his character. It worked! She experienced flashes of his prior 24 hours and pulled back her hand in shock as though she had just touched a hot stove. *"Todd Bristol?!"* she thought to herself.

Robert was wrong; this driver could not be trusted! She saw that this driver had placed listening devices in her hotel room and that he was collaborating with people in powerful government positions to keep tabs on her. One of these faces that flashed before her mind was that of the distinguished Brit she had just shared a flight with—Todd Bristol!

She knew that these people knew she had been contacted by those in the FDA who were against their schemes. They didn't know how much she knew, but that she was someone to watch. Esther suddenly felt betrayed somehow. Mr. Bristol had seemed like a friend. Next time she sees him she will be sure to look for an aura or find out about his last 24 hours!

Esther was tempted to change hotel rooms, but decided to let this play out. She also determined to find a way to tell Robert and Thomas about this double-agent driver that they "trusted."

"*What have I gotten myself into*?" she asked herself.

Chapter VIII

CLASSIFIED DOCUMENTS

The first thing Ester wanted to do once getting settled into her hotel room was to collapse into bed, or take a relaxing bath in the jetted tub, but she knew she needed to review the classified documents Robert and Thomas had given her.

Suspecting that she might avoid any potential cameras, she decided to review the files in the bathroom. So, she started the water and called her dad.

She told him about how the job interview went, and that she needed to rest up for the interview and the return trip home tomorrow. Esther knew how to compartmentalize her thoughts, so it was easy to laugh and behave normally for her father's sake; as well as for those who were listening.

After hanging up the phone, she began gathering things to carry into the bathroom. She scooped up the file with a change of clothing so that if there were a camera in her room, it would not be obvious that she was doing anything unusual.

The file began with a list of names. These were people she could "trust." Also included, was a list of names of people she needed to be careful of. The titles of those on both lists were impressively high. She quickly committed the information to memory and went on to the next page. She was grateful that she had a photographic memory. It really came in handy for tasks such as this.

Next was a report which listed that the number of American citizens with Cherokee blood who had been eliminated to date was almost 50,000! It showed that in the 2010 census, there were 819,105 people who stated that they had a Cherokee ancestor, and these people were all being targeted. It also listed 260,000 Cherokee tribal citizens. Each of these people were also targeted. That means, of the 323,000,000 people living in the United States, one out of every 322 people would be an instant target!

There were pages with the scientific information, including the special DNA markers, information about the various assortment of cancers that can be eradicated, and information about the tests and how this had been verified. It was suspected that some sort of method for finding individuals with these DNA markers was underway.

The file also included information about the testing that has been done, and also about the disease that has been administered to those who have been killed. Esther was impressed with the thoroughness of this report. Whereas most people would not make any sense of the statistical information, charts, tables, and numbers; they made perfect sense to her. Terrifying sense.

It was actually quite ingenious. The medicine itself didn't cause the issue, it was more like a binary effect of the medicine and the alcohol in cough syrup (or any alcohol for that matter) that caused an almost instantaneous blood clot that usually resulted in a coronary embolism. There had been some cases that resulted in massive strokes or pulmonary embolisms instead, but these were rare. Nevertheless, they both rendered the same result. Death.

Esther closed her eyes, shook her head, and took a slow breath. She was disgusted with the thought that people would actually be involved with something like this. Her heart filled with compassion for those who had been exterminated, and their families.

She slipped into the hot water and inspected the final page of the report. It was a simple page with the following instructions:

COMMUNICATION PROCEDURE

- View weekly classified ads from inanimate object names, i.e. chair, banana, car, etc. found in the National Enquirer.
- Messages are deciphered using the first book listed in the Washington City Paper classified section for the same week.
- 1st number is the page.
- 2nd number is the line on that page.
- 3rd number is the letter. Spaces do not count.
- Nonsense words are actually numbers. Decipher with the following key:
    - A=1
    - B=2
    - C=3 etc.
- To send a reply message, use the same book last used.
- Only ask to meet in an extreme emergency.

"It's essentially an adapted Playfair Cipher." Esther absorbed the seriousness of this task. "Why me?" she whispered to herself. She set down the pages, looked into the water at her reflection and softly asked again, "Why *not* me?"

She leaned back and closed her eyes, just for a moment. In her exhaustion, she fell asleep almost instantly. Strangely, she dreamed she was in some volcanic hot springs, looking at her reflection as she had just done. She touched her reflection to slap the water and make ripples, but was instantly pulled into the water.

She felt the familiar disorientation from the swirling lights and stars, gathered her senses, then studied her surroundings. She found herself sitting on a stump near a dirt road. At least she thought it was a dirt road rather than asphalt. There was nothing modern about the homes she saw. The surface of the road and surrounding earth was covered with what appeared to be a blanket of sparkling, white diamonds. Each reflection, a particle of glistening water that was singing praises to The Creator in delicious tinkling harmonies.

As Esther got up and began to look around her, she noticed a large wagon pulled by two black horses coming toward her. Sitting high above the horses was a man wearing a dark blue jacket with lots of brass buttons in two rows down both sides of his chest. There were two short stiff white collars sticking out near his neck and a red bow just below them, like a bow tie of sorts. There were also large brass buttons near the end of his sleeves and a strip of red. He was not clean shaven, and his gristly face, along with greasy hair, furrowed brow, and slumping posture told everyone around him that he didn't want to be there.

The wagon was loaded up with supplies. Attached to ropes on the sides of the wagon were some pots and tools, and a cage made of branches tied together that had some chickens crowded inside, and other household items as well which made a loud tinkling noise as it moved along the bumpy path.

As the horses strained to pull the load, Esther got a look at some of the items in the wagon. Not only were there barrels of food stuffs, but there were blankets, chests with personal items, a few sticks of furniture, and she could see a rocking crib for a baby.

A few other wagons followed with more provisions, but they also carried the very old, the very sick, and occasionally women with small children. Following behind these wagons was a large group of "Cherokee" (People of the Fire), or "Ana Shina'Abe" (People of Shinar).

Esther watched, speechless, as she saw some men wearing deer-hide leggings, hunting jackets, and turbans woven from leather and cloth. Younger men were wearing short tunics with a beaded belt around the waist, and coarse homespun pantaloons that were gathered at the ankles. Their heads were shaved except for a small patch of long hair near the crown where an eagle or turkey feather was tied to the "scalp-lock." Many of these young men had elaborate tattoos on their heads and arms.

Esther saw women wearing deerskin dresses with lots of long narrow fringe, shell and rope belts, and lots of draping glass-bead and shell necklaces. She also saw some women wearing dresses of cloth with puffed sleeves that consistently had three ribbon stripes sown into the bottom of the sleeves, again at the hem of their skirts, and on top of their shoulders as well.

Many of them wore a blanket about them like a cloak that served as a bed at night. The colors were vivid red, blue, and green as is the traditional tartan from Scotland. The Cherokee leader, Chief John Ross, was only one-eighth Cherokee (of the Bird Clan); his father was Scottish, and his mother was Scottish/Cherokee mix. The rest of his ancestry was from the highlands of Scotland. This would account for the colorful preferences of The People.

Alongside the wagons and the group of people, more men in uniform rode horses. They carried rifles and gruffly barked commands to the displaced civilization of families. Immediately behind the last wagon, tied to a line of rope, Esther was shocked to see some men with metal shackles on their ankles, their hands tied together, and forced to move at the pace of the horses. They appeared to have been battered, and were certainly exhausted as they forged miserably forward.

Most people wore leather moccasins. Some of these moccasins were gathered together on the top and looked more like a sock than a shoe. Others were decorated with beadwork on the top. Those who wore shoes had ornate stitching designs on the inside ankles. Esther was saddened and surprised to see that some people were only wearing rags on their feet, or nothing at all. It was then that she noticed red marks on the snow behind the sorrowful band like bread crumbs for someone to follow. "*Blood!*"

Then there was the sound! Thousands of people, crying as they marched mile after endless mile. Mournful crying. Sorrowful sniffles. Children, women, and even the proud men – warriors – broken spirits all crying as they pressed forward through endless exhaustion and humiliating submission.

A flood of compassion and overwhelming sorrow fell upon Esther as she realized that these were her ancestors. It brought the atrocities she witnessed to a more personal assault in a singularly penetrating way. Esther tried to control her emotions, but her chest was heaving and her face was hot as she fought back the tears.

She closed her eyes tight and shook her head. The next thing she knew, she was lying in the bathtub. She sat up with a jerk; the file folder now wet and running; the pages sticking together and print bleeding through in one thick mass.

"Well, I was supposed to destroy it anyway," she muttered to herself. She tore the wet clump of papers in small pieces and flushed them (along with her melancholy mood) down the toilet.

Chapter IX

MS. COLLINS

Esther arrived 10 minutes early for the interview and waited patiently for her meeting with Ms. Collins. Before long, a middle-aged slightly over-weight woman with long chestnut hair and a nice smile walked toward her. She wore blue flats, nylons, and a flowing blue skirt with a matching blazer. Her silk blouse had a floral pattern and large ruffles. She wore a step-tracking device watch/bracelet on her left wrist, a yoga bead bracelet on her right wrist, a large diamond wedding ring, but no earrings. Slightly visible underneath her blouse Esther noticed a Cherokee corn-bead necklace!

Slightly distracted, Esther stood to reach out for the handshake offered to her from the woman with stunning green eyes. Esther was almost entranced as she noticed the clarity of the color of her eyes, and the brightness of her aura. It was thick, white, bright, and had colors like a rainbow out on the tips of the radiating streams of light. She blinked her eyes and shook Ms. Collins' hand.

At that moment, the last 24 hours of this woman's life flashed immediately before Esther's mind. She had been looking through Esther's file. It had more information in it than Esther had thought was available online, so she felt quite exposed.

Esther could see that Ms. Collins lived in a small apartment with a lot of plants and artwork. Apparently, she was an artist and musician. There were lots of photo albums and books. She spent time in the morning praying, reading scriptures, and writing in a journal before getting ready for work. She wasn't on the list provided by Robert and Thomas, but Esther felt she could trust her so she smiled. Ms. Collins returned the smile and her face seemed truly radiant.

Ms. Collins invited Esther into her office. As they walked in, Esther was overwhelmed with the peaceful feeling she felt there. It was as tangible and refreshing as an ocean breeze, but was also comfortable and inviting as a cozy blanket in front of a fireplace on a snowy evening. An oil infuser puffed up a deliciously relaxing breath of frankincense just as Esther entered the room.

There were inspirational pictures and phrases on display, artifacts from international travel, and family photos. Ms. Collins' office had the typical mahogany desk with matching bookshelves. Esther sat across the desk for the interview feeling no nervousness whatsoever.

As they spoke, a gentle peace settled on Esther; much like the calm she felt whenever she played her mother's flute or sat on a beach listening to the ocean waves. She could feel her heartbeat begin to slow, and a contented harmony between herself and Ms. Collins settled in on the room.

"So, tell me… why should I hire you?" she heard Ms. Collins ask.

Esther felt as though she had been suddenly awakened and her mind was scrambling to know what to say. Ms. Collins obviously didn't know about the FDA and the corruption there, or did she? "*Does she know about the group trying to root out that corruption? Has she been told to hire me, no matter what?*" Esther thought quickly to herself.

Suddenly, Esther felt a warmth just over her right shoulder, as though someone were standing there, but obviously no one was... It was like an invisible person had placed a hand on her shoulder. The person seemed familiar to her. It felt like her mother, Ziven.

In that split second, Esther was left with a thought; a quote from Martin Luther King Jr. "*Courage is the power of the mind to overcome fear.*" Calm came to her again, and she responded serenely.

"I am smart and can figure out creative solutions to any problem I am faced with. As you know, I have a great deal of experience in the necessary sciences, and a talent for discovery.

"If you do choose to hire me, you won't regret it. You will be pleasantly surprised at the efficient volume of quality work you will receive from me. My attention to detail is exquisite, my integrity is impeccable, and one of my Master Research Theses was about how RNA and DNA is affected over time by available foods, environment, and the accessible gene pool.

"So, you see, I have a lot to offer this department."

Ms. Collins smiled. This young woman exuded a unique self-assurance, and there was something more; Esther intrigued her. Chloe continued to ask the other questions on her list as a formality, but she had already made up her mind. She nodded as she stood up with her outstretched hand. "Miss Cohan, I would like to offer you this position. You still have several other managers and directors to meet with, but if I have anything to say about it, you are my first choice."

"Thank you for your confidence. I guess we'll see how the other interviews go," Esther responded, shaking the director's hand vigorously. As expected, Esther was made instantly aware of further glimpses from the last 24 hours in Ms. Collins' life, which confirmed in her heart a compassionate concern for a woman who was genuine, good, and kind. She was also troubled, though Esther couldn't make out exactly what the problem was. She just knew that it was all-consuming and had something to do with Ms. Collins' children.

As Esther left her office, Chloe Collins closed the door, returned to her desk, and sat down and let out a large sigh. She had interviewed three other final candidates for this position, all were competent and capable, but who will actually get the job? The decision wasn't entirely up to her.

She liked Esther best. It wasn't just her experience, her resume, or even the interview they just had. There was just something about her that drew the soul toward her. Hopefully Chloe's colleagues will feel it too.

Chloe closed her eyes for a moment. She hadn't gotten much sleep the night before. Sometimes it's just difficult to turn off all of the information and stop worrying about things with her family, things at work, and things in the world long enough to actually relax and drift off to sleep.

As she took a slow, deep breath; a thought flooded her mind. "*Esther will be instrumental in bringing order and honor to many areas that concern you.*" This thought did not surprise her, but filled her heart with a profound feeling of peace and comfort. She nodded and responded with a heavenward prayer of thanks and took another cleansing breath and smiled.

Chloe reached over to the corner of her desk and picked up a framed photograph of her children. "*Perhaps Esther Cohan will be able to help us. Maybe we can trust her with our secret,*" she thought to herself. She stroked the images of the faces of her children with her thumb, drew the frame and held it close to her chest with her eyes closed. She furrowed her brow and took another slow, deep breath and lifted her chin heavenward, and then smiled serenely.

Chapter X

THE MALL

Esther decided to take a walk around The National Mall before returning to the hotel. It would give her time to think and to clear her head a little.

After leaving the Pentagon, she took a shuttle past the Arlington National Cemetery, over the beautiful Potomac River, and to the Lincoln Memorial. As she walked up the 58 large white marble steps, into the huge columned entrance and looked up into the face of the facsimile of the 16th President of the United States of America, she was filled with a profound respect for this man who stepped up to face the role of history he was met with – Abraham Lincoln.

As she walked around reading the many quotes engraved into the marble, one phrase seemed to stand out in glowing letters as she read it, each word lighting up in a smooth wave across the characters line by line. "*With malice toward none; with charity for all; with firmness in the right, as God gives us to see the right, let us strive on to finish the work we are in; to bind up the nation's wounds; to care for him who shall have borne the battle…*"—Abraham Lincoln

"*This is why you are here,*" a voice within her seemed to interrupt. Esther was left with a warm tingly feeling that started at the top of her head and flowed through every cell of her body confirming the truth of that statement. Esther knew it referred to her decision to help clean up the FDA covertly.

Another engraved quote from this sensitive man had the same affect. "*It is rather for us to be here dedicated to the great task remaining before us—that from these honored dead we take increased devotion to that a cause for which they gave the last full measure of devotion—that we here highly resolve that these dead shall not have died in vain—that this nation, under God, shall have a new birth of freedom—and that government of the people, by the people, for the people, shall not perish from the earth.*"—Abraham Lincoln

Immediately, Esther realized that the Cherokee people who have been killed in order to carry out corrupt plans of greed and conspiracy against the citizens of the United States, are the ones who have paid the "last full measure of devotion." She felt a growing passion for this cause. "*They shall not have died in vain*," she silently whispered resolutely to herself.

Esther walked through the Korean Veterans Memorial. A morning mist hugged the ground. The nearby trees not only served to seclude the area from the busy city, but kept the lawn shielded from the rising sun. The cool, moist air clung to the ghost-like statues of soldiers with moist cloaks as though they were literally canvasing the area. An eerie feeling came over her as she thought of the terrible conditions those who bravely defend this country must endure. Her heart filled with gratitude and compassion for the cost of their devotion. These were sacrifices like leaving their loved ones behind, not being able to see their children grow up, witnessing and suffering the trauma of war, loss of limb, loss of sanity and peace.

She slowly walked toward the unfinished statues of Martin Luther King Jr. that seemed to be literally emerging from the unhewn stone. Again, and again, the following quotes pulsed within Esther an increasing passion for justice; like a drumbeat mounting from deep inside of her.

"*I believe that unarmed truth and unconditional love will have the final word in reality. This is why right, temporarily defeated, is stronger than evil triumphant.*" – Martin Luther King, Jr.

"*Injustice anywhere is a threat to justice everywhere. We are caught in an inescapable network of mutuality, tied in a single garment of destiny. Whatever affects one directly, affects all indirectly.*" – Martin Luther King, Jr.

"*True peace is not merely the absence of tension; it is the presence of justice.*" – Martin Luther King, Jr.

"Powerful ideas," Esther whispered to herself solemnly.

Next, she walked around the beautiful Tidal Basin toward the Jefferson Memorial. The reflection in the water revealed a blue sky with a few fluffy cumulus clouds that were streaming rays of sunlight as the morning sun rose on the park. Sparrows and pigeons were beginning to scour the ground near every park bench for crumbs of food left behind by careless visitors. Esther could sense their excitement and anticipation as they searched for bits of food.

The sidewalk was lined with flowering ornamental plumbs. Their pink blossoms littered the walkway creating a magical arch. Esther could sense the joy of the trees as they felt her serenity. "*You are more loved than you know,*" they whispered to her as she walked among them. "*Thank you so much,*" she replied in her thoughts.

Upon reaching the 19-foot-tall memorial, Esther walked slowly up the wide steps toward the round, bright dome with white marble columns. Inside was a bronze statue of Thomas Jefferson.

Esther's heart was pounding in her chest now as her commitment and resolve grew fiercely inside her, rooting her feet deep below the surface of the earth and reaching far above her head through the sky like a pillar of light as she read the following quotes:

"*I have sworn upon the altar of God, eternal hostility against every form of tyranny over the mind of man.*" – Thomas Jefferson

"*We hold these truths to be self-evident: that all men are created equal, that they are endowed by their Creator with certain inalienable rights, among these are life, liberty, and the pursuit of happiness…*" – The Declaration of Independence

"*…Indeed, I tremble for my country when I reflect that God is just, that his justice cannot sleep forever…*" – Thomas Jefferson

Almost bereft of energy because of the emotional sensations of the morning, Esther made her way to the Holocaust Museum. Unfortunately, it didn't open until 10:00am, so Esther planned to return to it later. She made her way toward the monolithic white pinnacle surrounded by a circle of flags. As she sat on a nearby bench, she watched the flags. They were only slightly moving, but the pattern of their fluttering reminded her of ruffled dresses swirling as dancers spin and twirl.

Rays of the sun were streaming from behind the 555-foot obelisk giving it an air of the divine. Esther stood up and walked over to the behemothic memorial. As she reached her hand out to touch the huge, flat, white marble stones, she felt a bonding connection with the purpose for which this monument was constructed. The 37 years it took to complete it and the obstacles overcome to do so in memory of the father of this country, George Washington, is a call for us to remember who we once were, and who we must be again. A people who valiantly fight together against all odds, and sacrifice selflessly for what is right. The stone didn't exactly speak to her, but it did communicate with her a longing for a return to the foundational values that it represented. A longing to have so many sacrifices not have been given in vain!

Esther made a slight detour to the World War II memorial. Its perimeter was lined with an elegant representation of all 50 states, while in the inside perimeter were stars representing the more than 400,000 fallen heroes—"*The Price of Freedom*."

An old man in a wheelchair sat solemnly near the dedicatory wall with names of fallen soldiers from Montana. His wrinkled face almost hid his tear-filled eyes. A trembling hand rubbed a creased brow as the old veteran shook his head back and forth. Esther tried not to stare, but felt drawn into the emotion of the moment.

A teenage boy knelt by the side of the old fossil, looking up at him, and listening intently. Esther smiled. *"And the story is passed from generation to generation… as it should be,"* she thought to herself.

As Esther circled the pulsing fountain of water in the center of the memorial, she became aware of a young man with sunglasses, jeans, white Sketchers, an Under-Armor hoodie, and a NYU baseball cap leaning against a wall looking at his phone. She had seen him somewhere before. *"But where?"* she strained to force her memory to respond.

She tried not to stare, but something in her gut told her she needed to pay attention to see if this man, or anyone else were to ever follow her. A chill went up her spine and instantly she was anxious to get back to the hotel. Esther suddenly remembered that a bus would pick her up in front of the White House and go right past the JW Marriott hotel on Pennsylvania Avenue, where she was staying.

The wait for the DC Circulator was not long, and the cost was only one dollar. As she waited, a street vendor came by offering funnel cakes with everything from deep-fried Oreos, to hotdogs in them. She was hungry, so she ordered some fried apple tenders and looked around for the man in the baseball cap.

Not seeing him she relaxed and stepped up into the bus when it arrived. Startled, the mysterious man sat next to her and pretended to read a newspaper as he whispered to her. "Sorry to startle you. It's me. Robert." Then he glanced at her as he adjusted his sunglasses.

"Are you with us?" he whispered. She hesitated, amused by his 'cloak and dagger' mannerism.

"I know you haven't started yet, but they will offer you the job. This paper is your first communication. Are you in?" he whispered.

Esther smiled, shook her head and slightly rolled her eyes at his disguise. "I'm in."

Robert got up, left the paper folded on his seat, pulled on the cord, and walked toward the middle exit, grinning widely to himself.

Esther picked up the National Enquirer from the seat and found the classifieds section. Near the top on the left of the page was an ad from "Apple Appleton." It simply had numbers that were separated by comas. She tore out that section, folded it, put it in her purse, then she self-consciously looked around to see if anyone was watching her. Now, she just needed to find the free newspaper to find out what book these numbers speak to.

Chapter XI

THE LIBRARY OF CONGRESS

Near the hotel was a convenience store. Esther got off the bus and looked around in the entrance for a free paper. The display was empty. "Do you have any more of these?" she asked the cashier, gesturing toward the empty kiosk.

The tall Asian man behind the counter was built more like a Polynesian. He removed the ear buds from his ears and said, "Huh?"

"These free papers, do you have any more?" she repeated.

"Uh, I think there's one back there that someone left," he said, pointing to the heated glass case with rolling hot dogs in it.

Esther found the free paper, folded it and put it in her purse. Then, realizing that she was still hungry, and smelling the hot dogs, she decided to look around to see if anything sounded good. She settled on a Naked green smoothie and a cinnamon roll, then made her way back to the cash register. As she left the well-lit store and entered the dimmer lighting of the street, she became aware that a shadowy figure was standing near the wall smoking a cigarette.

A shiver down her spine and a sudden sense of urgency to get back to her hotel room came over her like a tidal wave. Esther looked around just enough to keep the potentially sinister person in her peripheral vision; to see if he were following her. He was.

She reached the elevator, heart pounding, and nervously pushed the call button again and again. She got her key card out of her purse to have it ready, quickly exited the elevator, and made a beeline to her room. Fumbling slightly to open the door, she closed it behind her and suddenly realized that she was shaking.

"*Do I actually want to get involved? Can I really live like this?*" she asked herself breathlessly.

She walked into the bathroom to splash her face with water. As she returned to the bedroom, she saw the Bloodwood Flute. She gently picked it up, took it out of the deerskin case her father had made for it, and plopped down on the bed.

After taking a deep cleansing breath, she began to play. The Bloodwood Flute sang out warmly and clearly. The small hotel room sounded like a great hall as the mellow tones bounced off the ceiling and echoed cheerfully. The room seemed to expand until the walls disappeared completely.

Esther seemed to find herself on a rock cliff overlooking a deep winding ravine. The salmon, coral, and rust-colored rocks provided a beautiful backdrop to the winding green river far below.

Ziven stood before her, wearing a deerskin dress with long fringe dripping from her arms and neckline. Her long light-brown hair was flowing in the breeze as the sun began to set, coloring the sky with complementary colors of peach, fuchsia, tangerine, lilac, lemon, and magenta against the red rocks of Dead Horse Point. The scene was surreal; it was like being in a movie.

Esther told her mother all about the interviews, about the FDA, and about the danger to the Cherokee people. She also told Ziven about the strange dreams she'd been having; always witnessing various stages of what appeared to be The Trail of Tears.

"Do you know why you were named 'Esther'?" Ziven began.

"Yes. Father told me it was because you liked the name so much."

"That's right. You remember the account of Esther in the scriptures?"

"Of course."

"I vowed that if I ever had the chance, I would be like her. Now it seems you will have the opportunity to be like her. Like Esther of old, you will have the opportunity to actually save *your* people – the Cherokee people."

Esther thought about that for a moment. "Do you think that's why I've been having those dreams?"

"I am not convinced that they are dreams. How sharp are the images? Can you remember the details clearly even days later?"

"Yes. It's like they are imprinted on my memory. I can close my eyes and remember every detail vividly."

Ziven smiled and said, "Then, they are not dreams."

"Not dreams?" Esther exclaimed.

"No. I think they are either visions or…" Ziven hesitated.

"Or what?" Esther asked.

"Well, there is one other possibility."

"What, Mother?"

"With your special gifts, you could actually be traveling."

Esther raised one eyebrow and asked, "Traveling?"

"… in time." Esther was in shock. "In any case," Ziven continued, "there's one thing to always remember."

"What's that?" Esther quizzed.

"Whenever a person accepts a mission in this life, every resource, every opportunity, and every needed thing will be made available for that mission to be accomplished."

"So," Esther stumbled over her words. "So, do you think I have accepted an assignment to help save the Cherokee people?"

"Yes. I do," Ziven answered. "Not only that, but I have a feeling we each agreed to do certain things in this life. We accepted the specific mission we would be faced with in mortality. Does that make sense?"

"Yes. I think I understand," Esther replied.

At that, the hotel room walls returned and Esther found herself alone, sitting on the bed holding the Bloodwood Flute. As soon as she oriented herself to reality, she picked up the free paper at her side and began searching for the first book listed.

"There," she said out loud. Then, remembering that her room was bugged, she made up something that could throw her listeners off of her trail. "There is that movie I wanted to see! Oh, darn! I'm going to miss it. Oh well."

Little Women by Louisa May Alcott was the first book listed. Esther grabbed her purse and made her way to the concierge, being careful to notice whether or not she was being followed. She was not. "Is there a library anywhere near here?" she asked.

The tall young man with a brown complexion and dark brown eyes stood behind the tall counter anticipating her question. His black hair was curly on top and cut short on the sides. Although he wore a buttoned shirt with a plain dark tie and a red suit coat, Esther could tell that he had a muscular build. He smiled broadly, exposing his straight white teeth and said smoothly, "Of course. Let me show you with this map." Then he impressively read, wrote notes, and pointed to things upside down as he showed Esther where she was and how to get to the library.

After finding the Library of Congress on Independence Avenue, Esther went through security, then walked into the large circular center to look around. The tall domed ceiling was impressively beautiful. Half-dome windows formed a ring around the center of the ceiling, and the oak wood cabinetry that lined the walls was over 40 feet tall. It was breathtaking! The library closed at 4:30pm, so she had plenty of time, but with over 130 million items, there was no way she could find the right book without help.

A short co-ed wearing jeans, white Sketchers, and a grey polo shirt with an official-looking logo walked toward Esther and whispered, "May I help you find something?" Her blonde hair was wavy and revealed darker roots beneath the tousled curls. Her eyes were overly large for her size, a beautiful azure color, and she had lash extensions that made her eyes her most stunning feature. She helped Esther find the book in 30 seconds flat! That had to be a record.

Esther thanked her, looked around, and seeing nothing suspicious around her, sat at a small table near an exit with her back to the wall so she could see anyone approaching her. She pulled out the piece of paper she had ripped out of the classified section and began deciphering the message.

Page 2, line 1, letter 9 = s
Page 4, line 5, letter 1 = m
Page 16, line 1, letter 21 = i
Page 17, line 7, letter 1 = t
Page 19, line 8, letter 7 = h

She flipped through the pages guessing at the next letters before confirming them with the code.

22, 2, 23. 25, 4, 4. 27, 3, 1. 29, 3, 1. 29, 1, 1. 30, 8, 1. 35, 4, 9. 5, 1, 2. 8, 6, 18. 10, 6, 1. 14, 4, 4. 17, 5, 9. 04.23 16.30

She scribbled the letters faster and faster, flipping through the pages, and glancing up and around her quickly. Surely everyone could hear her heart pounding in her chest! But, no. No one was aware of her, nor her anxiousness.

"Smithsonian Space" had to mean the National Air and Space Smithsonian Museum. The final nonsense words had to be the date and time: April 23rd at 4:30pm. That was two weeks from today; her mother's birthday.

"*I wonder how my father will feel about all of this...*" Esther thought to herself. At that moment, she decided she could not share this part of her life with him. Not only would he worry, but Thomas and Robert had warned her that telling *anyone* else about what is going on could put them in danger.

She quietly put the book away, smiled to herself, and glanced around the great hall. The balcony that lined the walls near the ceiling and small desks tucked into every available nook and cranny made it possible for people to hide away in a multitude of places. Esther decided not to worry about things she could do nothing about, sighed softly, and began walking back to the hotel.

She didn't notice the slender man standing in the shadows, waiting for her to leave the Library of Congress. Only the glow of his cigarette, or the slight hint of menthol smoke could have given him away. After Esther crossed the street, the figure dropped his cigarette butt, stood on it and twisted his foot. Then, stepping out of the darkness into the light of the corner street lamp, Todd Bristol carefully followed her.

Chapter XII

ROAD TRIP

The weeks seemed to speed by. There was so much to do! Chloe Collins had been authorized to offer the job to Esther Cohan. Her team was prepared to set Esther up with all the necessary training, network and software access, orientation information, and resources. All the introductory appointments were scheduled, her office space was ready, and she was scheduled to start on Tuesday, April 24th.

Chloe could hardly wait. There was something special about Esther. She really liked her. She wasn't sure what it was. It could have been that cool pie-shaped wedge of gold in her eye, or the fun blonde streak in her hair. Maybe it was her genuineness, or the fact that she was so brilliant. It could have been that she seemed to be intuitive and creative. She felt like Esther was someone she could be friends with; someone she could trust – something that doesn't come easily in Washington, D.C.

"Do you have everything?" Michael asked his daughter as he struggled to keep his composure. He had spent most of the day before—Ziven's birthday—making sure Esther's car was in perfect working order. This was his gift to both Esther and his beloved Ziven.

"Yes, Father. I checked the list twice," Esther grinned playfully. "*You are so cute!*" she thought to herself. "So, you will miss me?" she teased.

Clearing his throat, Michael answered, "Of course!" Then, he gently placed his hands on her arms, looked into her eyes, and said, "Your mother would be so proud of you! I…" He struggled to regain his calmness. "You are the only light in my life since my Ziven left. You are everything to me! I…" His grip tightened slightly, he gritted his teeth and forced himself to say what didn't come easily. "I love you!"

Esther, overcome with emotion, threw her arms around her father. Then, grinning from ear to ear and blinking away the tears, she whispered in his ear, "I love you too, Aba."

Esther was surprised at the depth of feeling she felt for this man. She knew that she loved him. She had always known. He raised her. He did his best under less-than-ideal circumstances. She knew he loved her too, even though he had scarcely said the actual words to her. He had his own special way of showing it, so she just knew.

Michael cleared his throat, forced himself to release the grip on his precious gem, and gently pushed her toward her car. "You should be on your way, pe-par-par." (That means 'butterfly' and was his pet name for his only living daughter.) Esther blushed, spun around and plopped into her VW convertible. She did have a long drive ahead of her, almost 3 thousand miles. She honked and waved as she drove off, excitement building up inside her, beaming from ear to ear, her pony tail flying in the wind behind her.

Michael watched his beloved daughter drive away and wondered if he would ever see her again. Tears began to burn his eyes before he blinked them away. *"Oh, Ziven, how I miss you! Our little girl has grown up. You would be so proud."* After a few moments, he turned slowly and sat in a darkened room for several hours without moving. Almost without breathing. He had no desire to be in the present, and his thoughts seemed to live in the past. That was his comfort zone – in the past with his precious Ziven. Did any other place or time actually exist?

The route out of San Francisco was a blur. Before she knew it, Esther was heading east on I-80 toward Salt Lake City, Utah. After skirting Sacramento, the drive over the Sierra Nevada mountains was beautiful. Esther smiled as she sensed the nobility of the Redwood trees and the laughter of the Quaking Aspens.

After about four hours, Esther needed to stretch her legs and get some gas. She stopped in Truckee, California at Donner Lake. The crisp clean mountain air filled her lungs with fresh life and the sensation of joyful praise. The deep blue water was soothing and seemed to be humming in swells of melodic praise to The Creator. A gentle breeze tickled the leaves of the trees along the perimeter of the lake like feathers ruffling their branches in joyous delight.

Esther took in a deep breath. The scent of pine, soil, water, wild flowers, and all kinds of foliage filled her lungs with perfumed air. The sensation of love and gratitude consumed her. How could it not? All living things around her were singing praise to The Creator. Their resonance washed over her like a wave of delicious harmony.

As she walked into the visitor's center of the "Donner Memorial State Park" she read plaques and displays about the ill-fated "Donner Party" who were trapped by weather during the winter of 1846-1847. The pioneer group was caught without sufficient provisions after leaving Independence, Missouri on their way to California. Their wagon train rolled across the Great Plains and through the Rocky Mountains, but was seriously delayed when a "shortcut" leading southwest became treacherous.

"An early severe snowstorm prevented passage over the High Sierra Mountains and forced the pioneers to spend the winter near present-day Truckee. 41 of the 89 settlers perished when their supplies and oxen were consumed. The desperate emigrants finally resorted to cannibalizing their dead friends and relatives to stay alive." As Esther read the display, a shiver went up her spine. "Those poor people!" she exclaimed under her breath. "How horrible! They must have been so desperate!"

She didn't have time for any of the other interactive displays of the visitor's center. She needed to get back on the road; she still had six hours before reaching Salt Lake City. The images and thoughts about what happened at Donner Lake over 200 years ago were still haunting her, though. She felt a tremendous compassion wash over her that would not soon fade.

The drive through Nevada's flat lands with its long straight and seemingly endless monotony was almost hypnotic. Blinking her eyes and shaking her head, Esther reached for the knob of the radio. Each station was country western music or talk radio. All she could do was shake her head and sigh. Then she resorted to rolling down the window and singing at the top of her lungs to stay awake!

As she finally approached the Salt Lake Valley it was 7pm. The sun was hanging low in the sky and a beautiful sunset was forming in the air behind her. As she pulled into the parking lot of a hotel in Salt Lake City, she turned around to see rays of sunlight streaming through bright orange clouds. The sky became instantly saturated with colors of fuchsia, peach, bright yellow, tangerine, maroon, various shades of purple, red, and orange. It was simply breath-taking!

"Beautiful!" Esther gasped. She turned to look toward the east and saw a surreal beauty. Mount Olympus raised upward over 9,000 feet. Its snow-capped ridges reflected the pink of the setting sun in a way that almost made it look like it was glowing. She turned back toward the sunset and it was even more spectacular. The colors were deeper and more intense than before. It was truly awe-inspiring!

Esther breathed a deep breath of contentment, then turned to check in to the local hotel. She was hungry, so after taking her luggage to her room, she decided to take a walk around the center of town to see if she could find something to eat.

As she walked up West Temple Street, she began to see several bright white spires piercing the evening sky. Curious, she continued in their direction until she found herself across the street from the structure. It was behind a tall wall alternating granite and vertical iron bars that took up the entire block.

Even though she was standing in front of a Denny's and the smell of prepared food made her mouth water, her curiosity was more powerful than her hunger. She would come back to get a bite to eat later. Right now, she felt drawn to see this beautiful building with hints of European Gothic structure.

As she entered the cast-iron gate, she was impressed at the beautifully manicured grounds. Raised beds of polished granite held small canisters that cast white lights on the trees. Beautiful tulips of all colors were accompanied by yellow daffodils, purple crocus, pink and blue hyacinth, bright orange begonias, purple pansies, pink bleeding hearts, and many other lovely flowers all carefully arranged beautifully. She could sense their songs of praise. Their chorus blended with the humming of the trees in what felt like a column of light thanking The Creator for their lives.

There were several buildings, all very interesting and beautiful. To her left was a visitor's center, but it wasn't the building that caught her eye. It was a huge window with a white statue standing in it. Again, her curiosity pulled her toward it like a flowing river.

There was something different about this place; a profound peace seemed to permeate every cell of every rock and plant in this area more than any other she had ever experienced. Curious.

Suddenly she noticed there were people walking around. It was as though she had been all alone before. Some of their auras were thick and bright. They reminded her of Robert, that tall guy who knocked on her door only a few months ago, and changed her life.

As she entered the room of the North Visitor's Center on Temple Square, she was astonished to see a miniature of Jerusalem in the center of the room. As she walked toward it, she paid attention to a family standing near the display. The mother was very pregnant, young, and radiant. The father was holding a young toddler that was writhing to get down. Three other children were near them. One pushed a button, then excitedly pointed to the red light that lit the Mount of Olives. The oldest child, a girl with long blonde curly hair, read the information about another point of interest and then instructed her younger brother to push the button. Squeals of delight could be heard above the ambient noise as the laser pointed to the Temple Mount.

Suddenly, one of the small children began humming a melody. This was not just any melody. This was the tune Esther had heard in her mind after her interview with Marie Florence in San Diego. *"But how could that be?"* Trying not to stare, Esther numbly watched the young child and enjoyed witnessing the innocence of youth.

The light emanating from this family was bright and thick, especially around the children. Esther could not always see auras, sometimes she could only see energy fields of people, and sometimes nothing at all. Of all her many spiritual and special gifts, this was one she could not control, though she wished she could.

As Esther looked around the room there were gathering places, an information desk, and large paintings. She walked along the wall looking at each of the paintings and reading the plaques. They were all about prophets of the Old Testament and New Testament. There were a few others she was not familiar with.

The Old Testament, of course, was debated ad nauseum by the men in the North Beach Chabad Synagogue in San Francisco where she and her father worshiped every Saturday since she could remember. The New Testament was not as familiar to her, but Esther had friends at school who called themselves "Christians." They were good people.

Next, she found herself ushered with a group of people into the area with the large white statue she had seen through the windows. The wall was painted with a mural of planets and solar systems. Everyone sat down on soft benches facing the large marble statue of Jesus of Nazareth.

Esther had heard of him. Christians believe He was the Messiah. Jews believe He was a great rabbi. She wasn't sure exactly what she believed. To tell you the truth, she hadn't given it much thought.

A couple of young women with thick bright auras, who were neatly and modestly dressed, addressed the group telling them that the voice they were about to hear represented the voice of Jesus Christ. Then a soothing male voice began, "I am the resurrection and the life. He that believeth in me, though he were dead, yet shall he live," the voice said.

At that point, Esther's mind began to think of her mother. It was as though her mother were behind her because she felt a strange sensation start at her head and drench her body down through her toes just as she thought she heard her mother whisper into her mind the word, *"Truth."*

She didn't remember much else that was said, except that Jesus was the "creator" of worlds without end. She found that to be interesting. "*I thought Jehovah was The Creator*," she thought to herself.

As she left the visitor's center, the sky was quite dark, but the magnificent granite structure before her with the six spires was lit up before her like an enormous 223-foot hedge. It was behind a rod-iron fence, so Esther could see the stained glass arched windows and lights within. The building reminded her of European cathedrals she had seen pictures of, but the feeling she was feeling at this time was something she didn't think she could ever forget.

A warm peaceful feeling filled her body from the feet up through and beyond her head. Again, the same word came to mind – "*truth*" – but this time it seemed to also mean "*pure love*."

Esther was so caught up in thought as she left Temple Square that she almost forgot to stop to grab a bite of food at the Denny's on her way back to the Sheraton Hotel on 5th South and West Temple. She was tired, and had a long trip ahead of her. She knew she would fall to sleep the moment her head hit the pillow that night.

The next day's travel looked much like the salt flats just west of the Great Salt Lake, but instead of flat white scenery, it was green. Long straight flat roads with no mountains, only slight emerald hills. The highway at times was narrow and ill kept. Esther could see the double yellow lines bounce up and down like a roller coaster in anticipation of her arrival.

After about seven hours, she stopped to get gas in Cheyenne, Wyoming. It was bitter cold. Her face seemed to freeze solid immediately as she stepped out of her car. That's when she overheard two teenagers nearby…

"Negative 20 degrees?! That's why my snot is frozen inside my nose!" the girl wearing pink cowboy boots, camouflage, and lace laughed unreservedly.

Then, the young man said, "Here. You want to see something cool?"

"Sure."

Esther was curious now, but tried not to look as though she were watching. It was bitter cold as her curiosity got the better of her. The young man ran into the convenience store and came back out with a steaming cup of hot water. He said, "Watch this!" as he tossed the water high into the air. Before it hit the ground, it had turned into snow and floated down like feathery rain.

"Wow!" the teenaged girl said, giggling and obviously impressed.

Esther smiled as she got back into her car. What she had experienced was more than science. She had heard the delightful tinkling sound of laughter as the water vapor changed into crystals of snow. The event had been fun for the particles of H_2O too!

She finally pulled into Omaha, tired, stiff, and ready for bed. She didn't even feel like eating, but maybe that's because she had been snacking on Pemican—nuts, jerky, and fruit—all day. She remembered stretching out on the bed, but didn't remember falling asleep.

"Hello Abba… I'm fine, just tired… Sorry I didn't call you last night, I fell right asleep… How are you?... That's good… Really?... Oh… Uh huh… Okay, I'll call you when I get there… I will…I love you…"

Esther quickly showered, then started the seven-hour drive toward

Chicago. She was a little worried since everything she had read about Chicago painted the picture of violence and crime. On the other hand, pictures she had seen were simply beautiful. She would just have to keep an open mind.

As she drove along on flat straight roads, she could see tall buildings grouped close together in the far distance. It reminded her of the Emerald City in a movie she had seen when she was a child. The song "Follow the Yellow Brick Road" came into her mind. This made her smile and made her feel like skipping. That melody always seemed to come to mind, as though it were her life's theme song!

The moment she checked into her hotel; Esther decided to walk around. Surprisingly, she didn't feel unsafe. In fact, she was overcome with the beauty of the buildings and her eyes were constantly looking upward.

The glass walls of every building reflected white cumulus clouds with flat bottoms floating effortlessly across the deep blue sky. Each towering building seemed to pay tribute to the building next to it by offering a corner or edge that was cut out at the same height as its neighboring sister.

The feeling Esther felt as she walked around was one of peace, respect, and welcoming love. As the sun went down, fire filled the sky, and was reflected on each of the mirrored walls around her. It was as though they were living trees expressing love and praise, not buildings built by man. It was uniquely beautiful.

As the sky got darker, Esther felt a sudden chill. Wind began to stream between the buildings from the nearby inlet of Lake Michigan. Before she knew it, all the shops around her began to close, and she hadn't eaten dinner yet! She rushed into the closest deli before they could lock the door.

"I think I'll try the Chicago Dog," she said, feeling adventurous. "And sweet potato fries," she added.

Esther was curious as she opened the paper wrapping to reveal a long hot dog on a poppy-seed bun with yellow mustard, chopped onions, sweet pickle relish, a dill pickle spear, fresh tomato slices, and a pickled yellow sport pepper. These were not food combinations she would have ever thought to put together!

As she took a bite, it was surprisingly delicious. She had to stop herself from eating too fast. She had forgotten how hungry she was and was considering ordering another one.

She looked up at the clock to see how much time she had before the shop closed, when a man bounded through the doorway, fighting the wind to close the door. As he removed his gloves and hat, he revealed thick tussled ginger hair that was wavy and longer on the top, but cut short near his ears.

His eyes were large and hazel; some brown, some gold, some green, and bluish around the edges of his pupils. His lashes were slightly darker than his hair, and very long. His broad disarming smile and laugh revealed straight white teeth and dimples in his cheeks. His aura was thick and white with radiating glimmers streaming from him in all directions.

As he hurried forward and removed a long blue knitted scarf from around his neck. It had a white "Y" on it. John noticed Esther gazing at him and smiled as he began studying the menu to order. Esther suddenly realized her heart was pounding in her chest and her mouth was hanging wide open! She looked away quickly, her face hot from blood rushing to her cheeks, and tried not to look any more foolish than she felt.

"*You've got to be kidding me*!" she chided herself. "*Gawking like a school girl*!"

Suddenly, Esther looked up to see John standing in front of her table. As she looked up, and the light from the street streamed in through the window and landed gently on her features. John was astonished. This woman was breathtaking! Her lips were smeared with mustard and a piece of relish, but she was stunning!

Her lips – they were full and round. They looked soft… Her skin – it was clear and smooth. It looked soft too… Her nose – it was straight and seemed to tip up just a bit at the end. Her hair – it was the most beautiful deep auburn color (except for a streak of blonde just at her left temple) and fell in gentle waves spilling around her face and over her shoulders.

Yes, yes, she was amazingly beautiful, but it was her eyes that captivated him and made time seem to stand still. Her eyes matched her hair! Well, that is, except for a pie-shaped wedge of gold in her left eye.

As John looked into Esther's face, he felt as though he were in a trance. He wasn't sure he was breathing… but he really didn't care one way or the other. He also wasn't sure just how long he had been standing there looking at this angel creature before him, but he didn't care about that either.

Then, there was that awkward pause when both of them realized they had been staring at each other, and although time seemed to stand still… it hadn't. They both sputtered unintelligible words. Then John broke the spell. "What is that you have there?"

"It's a Chicago Dog," she replied.

"Is it any good?" he ventured.

"I wasn't sure when I saw it, but I think it's delicious! I like the contrasts of spicy and sweet; and the crunchy vegetables blended with the softer ones. I'm not sure I'm wild about the poppy-seed bun. Perhaps it should be toasted so it doesn't get soggy." She suddenly stopped herself, realizing that she had spewed more information than she was being asked, and at a much faster rate than she intended.

John chuckled, turned to the young man at the counter who was impatiently waiting to take his order so he could go home, nodded toward Esther and said, "I'll have one of those."

Esther ate more slowly so she would have an excuse to see John a few more minutes which took some doing since she had wolfed down nearly half of the hotdog in 10 seconds, flat! She opted not to order the second hot dog but to work on her sweet-potato fries in slow motion, to take smaller bites and enjoy each morsel.

She was delighted when John asked if he could sit with her. "What does 'Y' stand for?" she asked, gesturing toward his scarf. "*Does it stand for 'yes'*?" she teased to herself, but didn't dare be so bold as to say that out loud.

"BYU," he replied sitting up a little straighter as he said, "Brigham Young University. That's a private school in Utah."

She could see that he was happy that she had noticed it. Then John began to look uncomfortable. "You've got a little bit of mustard..." he stammered as he pointed to her bottom lip. He reached for a napkin and began to wipe it off for her. Esther was stunned and just sat there like a statue, awkwardly smiling... and blushing.

After a few moments of talking about the weather, the café lights dimmed. Obviously, the employees wanted to close shop. Esther, flustered, quickly gathered her things together. "Nice to meet you!" she called out as she quickly darted out the door and into the night. It occurred to her that she might be safer if she had asked John to walk her to her hotel. But she really didn't know him, and she had behaved so foolishly that she was embarrassed. She just needed to get safely to the hotel and out of the cold wind.

That night was miserable! First her stomach began to tighten up into a tense ball, then she began to sweat and feel nauseous. Her stomach was rumbling with painful bubbles of gas. She sat on the commode breathing heavily and suffering the pains of diarrhea. Not long after returning to her bed, she ran into the restroom again... this time, to throw up!

Soon she was in the bathroom again, but this time, she wished she had a bowl, for she felt as though she would do both at the same time. Finally, still breathing heavily, and too weak to return to the bed, she laid down on the bathroom floor clutching her stomach in agony, and wondering if she would get any sleep at all. "*When will this night be over*!" she silently shouted as a cold sweat engulfed her and made her start to shiver violently.

Then, a thought entered her mind that made her want to laugh and cry at the same time. It was a terrible thought; an evil thought! "*If it was the Chicago dog, I wonder if John is sick too? I wonder if he is lying on the floor of his bathroom right now just as miserable as I am*?" She couldn't laugh, though she wanted to. She had to throw up again, but nothing came out! Her convulsing body just had to keep trying as it distracted her from her dastardly thoughts.

Eventually, after what seemed to be an eternity, the morning light streamed through her bedroom window and Esther realized that she had actually fallen asleep – if only for a moment. She calculated that she had probably received about three hours of sleep altogether,

Crawling across the floor, she climbed into bed, pulled her knees up to her chest while holding on tight to her stomach, and planned to sleep just a little bit longer. She was feeling a little better, but she had an 11-hour trip ahead, and she couldn't afford to be a drowsy driver in Washington, D.C. traffic!

She woke up with a start. "*What time is it?! How long have I been asleep*?"

Knock! Knock! Knock! Then, there was a rustling of the door as the maid came in when there was no answer. Startled to see Esther still in bed, the old woman in the grey dress with a white apron quickly backed out and apologized in a thick Mid-Eastern accent, saying she would come back later.

"It's already 10 o'clock?! I'd better get going!" Esther exclaimed. She was feeling much better, but still a little weak from the traumatic night before.

The drive from Chicago to Washington, D.C. seemed to go by quickly. She stopped briefly to enjoy Lake Erie near Toledo, and only slightly noticed the beautiful trees of the Allegheny National Forest. All she could think about was John, though. She didn't even know his last name, but it was fun to daydream about him. Esther smiled and sighed. Yes, it was fun to daydream about John…

THE SMITHSONIAN AIR AND SPACE MUSEUM

Esther walked through the glass doors, through security, and into the huge open area where a lunar module and small private planes greeted her. She walked to the left and entered the Boeing Milestones of Flight Hall. As she rounded the corner she was awe-struck by the size of the huge F-1 liquid fuel rocket engine.

She was reading about how it produced the 1.5 million pounds of thrust required to launch the giant 363-foot long Saturn-V rocket that took the first astronauts to the Moon six times from 1969 to 1972. The engine was 18 feet high, 12 feet wide with the chamber spanning 9.5 feet in diameter and weighing 18,616 pounds! Huge!

Suddenly, her thoughts were startled by the sensation that someone was watching her.

Across the room was a familiar figure wearing a long trench coat, reading a brochure. Esther rolled her eyes, shook her head, and began walking toward Robert. He immediately stiffened, his blue eyes wide, his thick eye brows raised high. She jolted and stopped dead in her tracks. She had forgotten herself for a moment. Robert's wide, panicked eyes looked around to make sure no one had noticed the slip.

He reached into his pocket, pulled out a small paper folded to the size of a quarter, walked next to Esther and began pointing up at the rocket engine as though he were saying something to her about it. "When I shake your hand, put the paper I will give you into your pocket. Then, after I leave, go to the restroom and read it there. Flush it and follow the instructions exactly. Do you understand?" Esther nodded. "Try to look natural, but notice if you are followed. Don't worry, you'll do great," he said, trying to reassure her. Then, he shook her hand and said quite loudly, "Nice to meet you," and left.

Esther remained in the area for a short moment, then made her way toward the studio model of the Star Trek Starship "Enterprise." Then she paused at the "Spirit of St. Louis" plane and made her way to the ladies' restroom.

As she entered the restroom stalls, she unfolded the paper and read the following: "*Meet me at the entrance of the Smithsonian Zoo here in D.C. at noon.*" She flushed the note and made her way to the Smithsonian's National Zoo & Conservation Biology Institute on Connecticut Avenue.

Robert met her at the entrance and greeted her with a big smile. She almost didn't recognize him! He was wearing glasses, a hoodie, jeans and high-topped tennis shoes that were not laced up completely. He paid her way and ushered her through the security entrance.

As they walked to the right toward the Asia Trail, Robert began to talk in hushed tones. "You okay?"

"Yes," Esther answered.

"Do you think you were followed?"

"No. I don't think so."

"Welcome to the team," he said with a chuckle. Then, he continued, "Thank you for joining us. This is—as you can tell—a highly sensitive operation, and we have to be careful not to tip our hand, or we will lose everything we've worked so hard for up to this point."

"How many people are involved?" she dared. "Is there anyone I can trust? What happens to me if I am discovered? Am I in danger? What about my boss?" The questions poured out of her like pressurized water from a crack in a dam.

"Ms. Collins does not know what is going on yet, but we are preparing to bring her on board. We are confident that she will be a supporter. All you need to worry about is following the instructions you receive through our communication methods. You will mostly be a courier for the evidence we need to stop the genocide of the Cherokee people."

A slight drizzle began to fall, so Esther sat down in front of the Panda bear paddock. "You okay?" Robert asked with genuine concern.

"Yes, but what if these people find out that I am part Cherokee?" she asked.

Robert took her by the shoulders, turned her to face him and said, "You are not alone! Do you understand me? Just follow the mission of each task and know that there are others around you watching your back to help you succeed. You will never be told about all of our people who are around you, just know that you are very safe!"

Esther melted into Robert's eyes. His long lashes were dreamy and the smooth colors of his hazel eyes were intense like a summer's sky. She blushed and smiled. "Okay. I understand." She was so distracted that she didn't notice whether or not she experienced the usual 24-hour replay when he touched her shoulders.

"*You are never alone*," echoed in her mind as though somewhere inside her, someone wanted to make sure she got that message.

She gathered her courage and asked, "Okay, what's next? What do you need me to do? What do I need to know?"

"To answer your first set of questions, it's not important for you to know how many people are involved, but suffice it to say, we've got top people on our side."

Checking to make sure no one was watching them, Robert continued. "You asked if there is anyone you can trust. Besides me and Thomas Jepson, the answer is no. Even if the person you may be talking to is on our side, someone else might be listening. Just assume you are always being watched. If you are discovered, I won't lie to you, you could be in danger, but remember that we have people around you at all times making sure you remain safe."

"There are people watching us right now?" she asked, looking around.

"Yes… always."

On an impulse, she flung her arms around his neck and planted a kiss on his cheek. Then, she pulled back and giggled. A stunned Robert just stood there, motionless. She shoved his shoulder. "To give them something to talk about," she teased with a cock of her head.

It was all he could do to not let on about how much he enjoyed seeing

Esther like this. She was playful and breath-takingly beautiful. He gulped and tried to focus. "Don't worry. It happens all the time," he said, raising his eyebrows, opening his eyes and his mouth wide in faked shock while shoving her back with his elbow.

Then, he continued more quietly. "No, seriously, we have to be careful even in wide open spaces. There are sonar long-distance listening devices that can pick up conversations from up to 300 feet away. They are easy to get and very inexpensive."

Robert stood up and took Esther's hand. She numbly stood and followed him as they circled back towards the entrance of the zoo. "The next step is for you to go to the Liberty Bell in Philadelphia. You'll stand outside of the building on the south side near the exit, looking in at the bell through the window this Friday at 3:30pm. Wait for someone to ask you if you know when the next tour is. Tell them that you don't know, you just got there. They'll say, 'Oh, then you'll be needing this,' and they'll hand you a small flash drive. Bring it to me right here next Saturday at 3:30pm. Clear?"

"Got it. Um, if my boss isn't on our team, how do I get the days off if I need to?"

"You'll have Friday off. It's already been arranged. We'll worry about the rest when we get there."

As they made their way toward the zoo entrance, Esther's shoulder was bumped by a man wearing sunglasses and a hoodie, baggy jeans, and bright yellow sketchers. In that instant, she saw his last 24 hours of activity. He was handed a pistol, ammunition, and a thick envelope of cash by a man in a suit. He was shown a picture of another man in a suit and told to find him at the zoo at this time.

Esther stopped suddenly. Gasping and wide-eyed, she turned to Robert and whispered, "That man…"

"Who?"

"The one in the hoodie and yellow shoes," still whispering. "He's here to shoot someone."

Robert looked at her with raised eyebrows in confusion and concern. "Shoot who?"

Blinking her eyes and shaking her head Esther whispered, "I don't know." She closed her eyes tight and concentrated on the picture she had seen. "The man in the grey suit had reddish hair cut with a crew cut, average build, a square jawline, and a dimple in his chin. I know I've seen his face somewhere before, but I can't place it!"

"How do you know this?" Robert asked her. Esther was pacing now like the large cat in the cages they just passed.

"Look! I'm telling you, he's here to kill someone!"

Robert grabbed her shoulders and pulled her to him, then whispered in her ear, "We can't do anything about it. We can't risk anything happening to you. And without knowing who it is they are after, we can't help."

"But…"

"I'm sorry. We need to go. We need to go now. We can't risk blowing our cover."

They walked silently to Esther's car. "Cute car," he broke the silence.

"Thanks," she said numbly.

"Look, you will need to get used to using public transportation, or taxis when you are on a mission. This car makes you too easy to follow. Do you understand?"

"Yes, I guess so."

As she got into her car, Robert closed her door and leaned in as she opened her window. "Can I ask you a question?"

"Sure."

"How did you know about that guy?" he asked, peering deeply into her eyes.

"Sometimes I can see the last 24 hours of a person's life when I touch them."

Robert thought a moment, then said, "So, what do you see when you touch me?"

"The same."

"Interesting," he said—with a sideways grin and one raised eyebrow. Then with heart pounding he reached in, put his fingers through her hair to hold her neck, and kissed her gently on the cheek, and was gone.

That evening, Esther returned to her hotel room, popped a bag of popcorn in the microwave and flipped on the TV hoping to distract herself from thinking about Robert and John. It was the local news. She sat up with a start. Not because her popcorn was burning, though it was, but because she recognized the man on the news. "*It's the man in the grey suit with reddish hair in a crew cut, a dimple in his chin, and a square jaw line that I saw in that flash at the entrance of the zoo!*" she thought to herself.

Listening intently now, she didn't realize her mouth was gaping open and her eyes were wide in shock. "…where an unknown shooter somehow got a gun past security and shot Mayor Stevens three times before escaping. This led to a high-speed chase that ended in the perpetrator's vehicle (which had been stolen earlier that day) crashing into the concrete barrier and bursting into flames. The identity of the gunman has not been determined yet, nor the reason for this sudden attack. No one has stepped forward to claim this attack. Mayor Stevens had been visiting the zoo to see the new baby Panda Bear born in captivity. He was there with a group of school children from the local Leif Nelson Elementary School. Mayor Stevens was rushed to Mercy Hospital where he is currently in critical condition. It is unknown whether he will survive the surgeries needed to save his life. More details will be given as this story develops. No one else at the zoo was injured."

Esther sat back. "Wow!" she breathed heavily. Then, suddenly realizing the smell of burnt popcorn, she jumped up, pulled out the smoking bag, set it in the bathroom sink and poured water on the smoldering mess. She opened the window a crack, and went to open the door as well to try to fan out some of the choking stench.

When she opened the door, she gasped! Standing there was Robert, with his finger drawn up to his lips, telling her to be quiet as he looked around the room quickly. He motioned her to enter the hallway with him, which she quickly did.

They both began speaking at once. "It was the mayor!" "Have you seen the news?" Slowing slightly, Esther took a steadying breath then began. "Yes, I saw the news. It was the mayor that I saw in that flash at the zoo."

Robert gently took her shoulders and looked into her eyes. "Did you see anything else? Did you see anything that could help us know who was involved and why?"

Esther furrowed her brow and blinked her eyes as she was trying to recall that flashing moment earlier in the day. Although she had a photographic memory, it seemed that when it came to these flashes, there were so many disjointed segments and the flashes didn't always seem clear.

Shaking her head, she said, "All I remember is that someone handed him a thick envelope and said he would get the rest after the job was completed. I can't quite make out the face of the person giving the money, but I remember a man with a dark suit, red tie, and a tie clip…"

"Anything else?" Robert asked.

"The tie clip was unusual. It looked sort of like a sunflower and an ear of corn," she said, puzzled. "I have no idea about what it means."

Robert turned and began to pace. "The corn could be the Cherokee People because of the Trail of Tears and the legend of the corn beads." Esther nodded; she was certainly familiar with the story.

In the 1800's, when the Cherokee people were driven out by force to walk thousands of miles, about one third of the people died along the way due to exposure, malnutrition, and hardship. It is said that the bloody footprints that were left along the way effected a certain variety of corn plant such that its kernels were transformed to express their grief at what they were seeing take place. Their seeds became tear shaped and adopted a sorrowful shade of grey. The Cherokee people make necklaces out of Corn Beads that now grow wild along the infamous path called The Trail of Tears.

Robert continued, "The sunflower could represent the flower of new growth that grows taller than the other flowers, gives beauty and healing oil. These flowers also bow to the sun."

Esther looked at him quizzically. He turned to her to explain. "There's a faction within the opposing organization that has secretly sworn to do the dirty work of making sure this cause fails. That way, those involved within the government cannot be directly connected to the corruption."

Robert could see that Esther was beginning to feel fearful, and that she needed to know more so she would feel safe. "Mayor Stevens is one our people."

"But he wasn't on your list…"

"Nope. He wasn't."

Esther began to sweat and feel clammy. Her head started to feel light and tingly. "Are you okay? Do you need to sit down?" Robert asked. Then, in an attempt to reassure her, he said, "Mayor Stevens is okay. He's going to make it."

"Am I in danger too?" she asked with wide eyes and anxiety like a little girl longing to feel safe.

"Yes and no," Robert answered. Esther blinked her eyes and frowned in confusion. "You could potentially be in danger, but we are doing everything we can to protect you. I realize that might not seem like much after what just happened, but you have to trust me. You do trust me, don't you?"

"Of course!" she answered far too impulsively for her own comfort.

"You try to get some sleep tonight. After work tomorrow, meet me at the front lobby of Mercy Hospital. I'll introduce you to the mayor if he's up to having visitors."

"Okay," she hesitantly answered, smiled, and returned quickly to her hotel room.

Chapter XIV

MERCY HOSPITAL, WASHINGTON, D. C.

Robert escorted Esther past the security guards and into a hospital room on the top floor of the massive building. The scent of a variety of flowers jumbled together and seemed to float on the air filling the entire floor with sweet and spicy aroma. Mayor Steven's room was filled with flowers and looked more like a mortuary than a hospital room. He lay there still as death, with tubes connecting him to several machines; beeping and monitoring his every vital sign.

Looking at him with compassion and concern, Robert approached his mentor and gently touched him on the shoulder. Mayor Stevens slowly stirred, blinked a few times, and smiled in greeting. He took a slow deep breath and then opened his eyes wider to focus on the beautiful woman standing at his old friend's side. Then, with a quizzical look, he frowned at Robert.

"This is Esther Cohen, Mayor. She is our only and best hope," he began. As he placed his arm around Esther's shoulder, she could instantly see a flash of the last 24 hours in Robert's life. She saw him rising early to study scriptures, then go for a jog in a park. She knew he was a Christian and that he spent time praying for Mayor Stevens and for her as well. Slightly distracted by that thought, she forced herself back to the present.

"Pleased to meet you," she said as she reached out her hand. Careful not to take it too firmly, but not being one to give weak handshakes either, she turned her palm down so she could grip his fingers determinedly without hurting him. Then, at that instant, she saw a flash of the last 24 hours for this man as well.

Mayor Peter Stevens was a soft-spoken man, diminutive in stature and sweet in spirit. He liked to follow the same pattern every morning in honor of his deceased wife: kiss her picture, greet the sunrise with a cup of coffee and a commitment to serve someone that day in her behalf. That day, he had decided to select one of the elementary school children at the zoo to quietly pay for a year's worth of lunches. He hadn't made up his mind which child to select yet when a bullet suddenly hit his left shoulder forcing him backward. Another painful tearing of flesh could be felt in his upper arm as he swung around. And finally, another shot ripped through his side and out his back as he fell to the ground, puncturing his lung in the process.

In that moment, Mayor Stevens had several thoughts go through his mind instantaneously. *"Is this it? Will I see my beloved Patricia soon? I wish I could have selected a child to help before this happened! What will happen to the Cherokee people?"*

Not knowing how much time had passed, and embarrassed in the event that it was longer than it should have been, Esther quickly released the old man's hand, looked down, and blushed. Robert watched her intently and smiled.

Totally unaware of what had just happened, Mayor Stevens cleared his throat and asked in almost a whisper, "So, you are the one I've been hearing so much about."

Esther shot Robert a questioning glance. Then Mayor Stevens continued, "Thank you for joining the team. I look forward to..." and with that he drifted off into a medicinally-induced deep sleep.

Robert gestured for Esther to follow him out into the hallway. When they were quite alone, he said, "I'm going to ask you some questions. Please keep looking forward and try not to make any facial expressions in case anyone is watching... and they are always watching. Got it?" She nodded. "Just say uh huh or uh uh. No nodding. Okay?" "Uh huh," she responded while continuing to look ahead. Inside, she was wondering why all the cloak and dagger. Surely, if she were being watched, it was known that she had visited the mayor.

Robert began, "I have a personal question to ask you, but it also affects the cause. Okay if I begin?"

"Uh huh."

"Does it happen every time you touch someone?"

Esther stopped and looked at Robert in surprise, then remembered what he had said and continued walking, looking straight forward. "Uh huh."

"Wow! What do you see? How much do you see? What's it like?"

Esther rolled her eyes and kept walking without responding. "Oh, sorry. Listen, I need to prepare a place where we can talk safely. Okay?"

"Uh huh."

"I'll place an ad in the usual place. Can you get home alright?"

"Uh huh."

"You will be followed by one of my men to make sure you get there safely. Are you sure you can manage?"

"Uh huh."

"Okay, then. See you soon!" And with that, Robert turned to the left, rounded a corner, and was instantly gone.

Esther wondered about sharing her secret. Did she trust Robert enough to tell him? She hadn't told anyone before, not even her father. What if Robert didn't have authority to keep her from becoming some sort of "secret weapon" that the government would exploit? What if all of this got out of hand?

She thought about Robert as she rode the bus and continuously until she entered her apartment. She hadn't paid attention to see if anyone was following her. She barely remembered how she even got home. Time seemed to float in a rolling fog like a San Francisco morning. Before she knew it, she was drifting off to sleep with the image of Robert's face underneath her eyelids.

Chapter XV

THE DEPARTMENT OF FORENSIC SCIENCES

As Esther entered the tall glass building and was greeted by a security scan, she showed her new name badge and promptly made her way to her office where she found Chloe Collins, the HR Director who hired her, waiting. Her aura was layered tightly around her like an onion. It was still bright white, but something was obviously deeply troubling her.

Esther greeted her with a handshake which revealed that Chloe had spent most of the morning crying and pacing until she finally went to her knees to ask for help. At that point, she had a thought that talking with Esther would help solve her problem.

Esther smiled, sat down at her desk, and gestured for the senior manager to have a seat.

"Where to begin…" Chloe thought to herself. "Um, you're probably wondering why I am here," she began weakly.

"The thought had crossed my mind," Esther replied honestly. "Can I get you a cup of coffee or anything?"

"No… Thank you…" Her hesitation began to feel awkward, then

she finally began to speak very slowly; as though she were repeating well-rehearsed lines.

"I've been watching you ever since that first interview. You are a very deep thinker, and you truly care about people." Cloe looked up at Esther, gathered her courage to continue.

"I feel I can trust you." She looked up again, searching desperately for some confirmation in Esther's eyes.

Esther smiled – trying to not reveal anything – and said, "What can I do for you?"

"In my position, I come across confidential information all the time. It is crucial that I keep confidences and practice exquisite integrity. To break that trust would lose me more than my job. Do you understand?"

"I think so," Esther answered patiently, but puzzled.

"Did you know that I have two beautiful children?"

Esther smiled and nodded, remembering the family pictures in Chloe's office.

Chloe closed her eyes, took a deep breath and began to plow through. She told Esther all about how she had been married to the Chief of the Cherokee Nation. They had two children together, a boy and a girl. Then a renegade faction within the Cherokee Nation Government threatened to kill the "half-breed" children and remove her husband from his council seat. Chloe had the option to take her children to a special monastery in Mexico for their safety, but she was not to ever see them again until they became of age. Her secret was exposed and her husband assassinated. Now her children are in danger from inside the Cherokee Nation itself.

"But that's not all," she paused briefly to gather her resolve, knowing what doing so might mean, and continued. "As I said, I see a lot of information and have pieced together information about the SolMaize organization and their plans to exterminate all people with the Cherokee DNA marker because they believe the key to cure all cancer is found in the DNA and RNA of those individuals. I also have identified several key players. They have infiltrated the FDA and the Federal Government at the highest levels."

Chloe looked at Esther, who was taking it all in, to assess her feelings about all of this. Determined to finish, she continued.

"I have also identified several individuals who are working to stop this madness. They call themselves simply 'The Resistance,' and I know that they have recruited you."

Having come this far, she committed to lay all of her cards on the table, and continued without looking back.

She told Esther that the renegade faction was being used by the SolMaize organization to help identify and hunt down all Cherokee people who were not pure blooded. They play to the arrogance and single-mindedness of the group, and hide the fact that they are actually searching for all people with any Cherokee blood.

"I have information that can help you. I am also in a position to keep an eye on critical operations and give an early warning if necessary. I only want to protect my children! I need to bring my children home and keep them safe. Can you help me?"

Esther took it all in. She noticed the aura around Chloe pulse and glow brighter and brighter as she spoke. Esther knew she didn't have authority to make any decisions for The Resistance. She also knew that she could trust this woman who obviously risked everything to bring her this information.

"I can't promise anything because it's not my decision to make, but I will see what can be done."

At this, the round woman jumped up as though she had just sat on a spring, bounded around Esther's desk and gripped her in a bear hug embrace. With tears suddenly flowing like a snow-fed spring waterfall, she sniffed and managed a muffled "Thank you!" and was instantly off.

"Well, I guess I won't have any trouble getting time off work for the cause!" Esther said to herself.

Chapter XV

PHILADELPHIA

Friday morning, Esther found herself in Philadelphia. It was a beautiful crisp morning and she had finally gotten a good night's sleep. She felt rested and excited.

As she made her way to the Liberty Bell Center in Independence National Historical Park on Market Street to see the Liberty Bell, she forgot to look behind her to see if anyone was following her. That was a mistake.

Esther walked around to the south side of the building which housed the Liberty Bell and looked for the exit near a large window. She stood there looking in at the historic bell with people surrounding its massive curves. She thought about the large crack and the physics involved in creating such a fissure.

Esther found her mind entering into the very molecules of the bell cast three times by John Pass and John Stow in the mid 1700's. The bell with the profound words imprinted upon its side, "Proclaim Liberty Throughout All the Land unto All the Inhabitants thereof." actually communicated with her. The pride that the tin, copper, gold, silver, arsenic, zinc, and lead elements of this historic bell had in creating the rich E flat tone for over 90 years as it called legislators to meet and warned the historic townsfolk in times of trouble was evident. Their sorrow at no longer being able to hold together to sing was distressing. She learned that there were some flexible deformations at temperatures that were low enough that the atoms could not rearrange during the strengthening phase of the bell's creation. The side effect of this was that the metal became more brittle and many small hairline cracks began to form. Over the years, the cracks grew. Now, the main crack is 24 1/2 inches long and half of an inch wide. The entire bell is 12 feet in circumference and three feet tall. So much beautiful depth of feeling resided in the very particles of this famous bell.

Lost in thought, she didn't notice that a man had approached her until the blind man tapped her foot with a long white cane. This startled her a bit, so she stepped back and said, "Oh, please excuse me."

The tall distinguished-looking gentleman with salt-and-pepper hair wore dark sunglasses and what appeared to be a very expensive grey suit. "Please don't be alarmed. I may not have eyesight, but I do have vision," he said cheerfully.

Stunned, Esther tried not to stare, but was impressed that a man with no sight seemed to be so confident and put together. She imagined what his life might be like, and wondered what happened to cause him to lose his sight, and how he learned to do even basic things like getting dressed, eating, or finding his way around Washington, D.C. of all places. She looked at him again and thought, *"Sometimes you have to look with more than your eyes to see."*

"Do you know when the next tour is?" he asked. Startled out of her thoughts, she wondered if this were her contact. "Uh, I don't know," she stammered. "I just got here."

"Then you'll be needing this," he said reaching out his hand as though he were going to shake hers. As she took his hand, he shook hers firmly and left in it a small electronic device the size of a bean. In that instant, as their hands touched slightly, the past 24 hours of Jeremy Benjamin's existence raced through her mind.

She saw exactly what life was like for this retired CIA operative. She saw the precision with which everything in his life had to be organized, simply to navigate. This man obviously continued to feel passionately about his country and wanted to fight its corruption to his very last breath.

Perhaps he could no longer serve the way he had in the past, but he definitely did have the vision to see a better future.

Esther tried to nonchalantly place the small flash drive in her pocket. Before she knew it, the blind man was gone and she was left standing alone in the crowd. Fighting the urge to spin around, she looked at her watch. It was 3:45pm. Most things in Washington, D.C. closed at 4pm.

She didn't need to be back to the airport until the next morning, so she decided to do some sightseeing while in Philadelphia. "I wonder if there is time to see Independence Hall?" she said out loud to herself, as she turned to walk south toward the building where the Declaration of Independence was signed centuries ago.

In doing so, she literally bumped into a person standing right in front of her. "Oh, excuse me!" Looking up, she recognized… "Todd Bristol?" He smiled and let out a guffaw. "I saw you standing there," he began, "and thought I'd say hello."

What he didn't know is that when she bumped into him, she saw everything.

She saw him following her and waiting for her. She saw a SolMaize tattoo on his left wrist when he had adjusted his watch earlier. She saw him make a phone call to someone reporting that he was "positioned to eliminate the threat." But the thing that shocked her the most, and made it difficult to control her reactions was that she saw that he had literally picked her pocket when they bumped into each other, and stole the flash drive she had just received!

Thinking quickly, so as to not show any reaction, she smiled nervously, made small talk, and tried to formulate a plan. A plan to retrieve the flash drive without being detected. But how?

"Would you like to walk with me over to Independence Hall?" she asked playfully. Caught off guard, Todd agreed.

The cobblestone sidewalks and streets were so charming and welcoming. There was a feeling in the air of stoic civic pride. The red brick buildings with white trim seemed to stand as witnesses to the great events that happened within their walls.

Esther wanted to enjoy all of these thoughts, but she had to act fast and smoothly. In her mind, she had seen Todd put the flash drive into the right pocket of his suit coat.

They passed a street vendor, and Esther got an idea. "Ooh, a smoothie would be delicious about now! What do you think?" she said as she bounded toward the street vendor. Todd followed tentatively. As he approached Esther, she pretended to stumble and spilled the slushy on the right side of Todd's suit.

Laughing and apologizing, Esther tried to brush off the flavored ice that was sticking to the fully canvassed $3,000 silk suit. Todd had to admit that the attention from such a young and beautiful woman was distracting. He didn't care about his suit. It could just go to the cleaners.

John Michaels sat alone in an out-door café Market Street in Philadelphia enjoying a delicious, dripping Philly Cheesesteak sandwich and staring off into the distance. He could not get her out of his mind. Even with all of the Naval EOD training, psychological preparation, and personal conviction, he could not quit thinking about the beautiful ginger he had met in Chicago months before.

He chuckled to himself as he remembered eating a Chicago Dog with her, and how violently ill he had been that night. *"I wonder if she got sick too,"* he thought to himself. He sketched in his mind the color of her long deep copper-colored hair with that gorgeous blonde stripe near her left ear. Then, there were her eyes. Those stunning eyes that seemed to match her hair… all except for that fascinating golden pie wedge. Mesmerizing.

He sighed deeply, shook his head, and came back to the present. Looking up and across the street before him, he had to blink. Was he imagining things? Like an angel chorus singing in a chick flick, he saw the sun gleaming off of Esther's hair as she flung it over her shoulder and walked without a care down the street looking up at nearby buildings and down at the tourist guide in her hands.

Instantly, and before he could impulsively jump up to greet her, the hair on the back of his neck began to stand on edge. Adrenaline pumping as he scanned the scene. Sure enough, about 100 feet behind Esther was her shadow. John didn't recognize him, but sensed he was trouble. He scoured the area to search for any other unfriendlies, but only saw the one.

He jumped up, dropped a handful of bills on the table, and hopped onto his motorcycle in one smooth move. He hoped Esther would comply with his plan, for her own safety, as he pulled up to her side.

"Esther, isn't it?" he jovially greeted her. Surprised, she stopped dead in her tracks. His eyes got wide as he whispered through gritted teeth loudly enough to be heard above the roar of his emerald-green Kawasaki Vulcan 900 cruiser. "You need to come with me… NOW!"

He grabbed her around the waist and threw her onto his motorcycle in one smooth motion. The strength of his arms caught Esther off guard. She held onto his waist and felt the hard, muscular frame of the man who was whisking her away like the hero in one of those silly spy movies.

In the moment they touched, Esther experienced that familiar flash of the last 24 hours of this man's life. She saw him wake up with a familiar nightmare, go running in a park, then calm down with Tai Chi. She saw him writing in a journal, researching his ancestors online, and praying for a long time. This touched her. Then, she saw him eating a Philly Cheesesteak sandwich while thinking of her.

Esther felt somewhat guilty at being privy to such personal information. But, at the same time, it created an instant bond and familiarity that would not be created in any other way. It was actually quite enticing.

The moment they sped off, three men dropped what they were doing and began to run after them. Two hopped into waiting cars, and a classic car chase ensued.

Motorcycles are more mobile in heavy traffic, but Esther was amazed at the persistence and tenacity of those following them. John kept looking behind him as he turned down side alley-ways and obscure streets, racing to get away from their pursuers. Esther held her breath as they bumped down a steep flight of steps, shouting for startled pedestrians to move out of their way.

As John and Esther ran a red light, a garbage truck blared its horn. The motorcycle began to skid sideways. Esther held her breath and closed her eyes tight. If this was the end, she didn't want to see it. John righted the bike and continued without slowing a bit. This made Esther hold on even tighter to John's firm torso.

Their chasers were still following them until John found a narrow alleyway that got even more narrow as they barreled down it with the remaining car in hot pursuit. Miraculously, the car actually got jammed between the walls, leaving John and Esther to continue at a normal speed.

John turned his head slightly, "You okay?" All she could do was nod. "You can breathe now!" he teased. John was right. Esther was still sort of holding her breath. She smiled weakly and asked, "How did you know, I mean about…?"

"I didn't," he replied. "I just had a feeling when I saw you."

The next few moments were silent as they drove down a beautiful city street with an entryway of branches and green foliage over-arching them, welcoming them. They stopped at Franklin Square, just north of Chinatown. John took Esther's hand and quietly walked her over to a park bench near Franklin Fountain. They sat there for several minutes, not saying a word.

John began, "So, why do you think those men were after you?"

Esther sized up John to see if she could trust him with her secret. She gazed into his intense hazel eyes, enjoying his long lashes, his thick aura, and his deep dimples. Then, she simply shrugged.

John was sizing up Esther as well. *"She is truly beautiful!"* he thought to himself, then literally snapped his head to get back to the business at hand. He ventured carefully, "What do you know about SolMaize?"

Esther caught her breath, then turned slowly to look at John. "You know about SolMaize?"

John began telling her about how after he retired from military service with the Marines in the bomb demolition unit, and had served as a personal body guard to several presidents of the United States, he was approached by The Resistance. "You may not realize it, but you are the lynch-pin in this entire mission."

"Why me? I'm nothing special."

John was astounded by that comment. Not only was she important to the success of the mission, she was becoming quite important to him personally as well.

Nodding to her pocket, he said, "That information you are holding has to be safely delivered tomorrow afternoon in order to save tens of thousands of lives. Each transfer of information has that potential."

"But why didn't they just ask someone like you – someone who has been trained – to do it? Why did they ask me? What's special about me?"

There! She had said it again! John wanted to tell Esther exactly what was special about her; exactly what he thought of her. But he couldn't. Not yet. It would cloud up the mission, and the mission must always come first.

"There are many who believe in the power of diversion. You have no idea how many times nuclear technology and other dangerous prototypes have been transported across the nation in the trunk of the car of some small-town hick or a simple minivan to avert suspicion." After the shock wore off and her face and her expression changed to comprehension, he continued.

"You have the real information, but I don't feel comfortable just letting you wander around without some sort of protection. If it's alright with you, I'm going to ask to accompany you for all future missions." He had hoped that Esther wouldn't mind. Her body language seemed to reflect that she was at ease with the suggestion.

Esther smiled to herself as she remembered how she retrieved the flash drive Todd Bristol had lifted from her pocket. She was successful, but he had been very smooth! As capable as she felt, she felt more comfortable knowing that John would have her back going forward.

As the two of them stood up to leave, a deafening crashing sound startled them. John knew that sound. It was the blast of a hand grenade! He instinctively reached out to cover Esther and shield her from injury with his body, but she wasn't there!

Esther had heard the blast. It instantaneously startled her and scared her to the very core. Suddenly, it was as if time stood still. That is, for everyone and everything except for her!

She glanced around at the water falling in the beautiful Franklin Fountain. It hung in the air, still as a photograph. She touched some of the sparkling droplets with her hand and left a space in the path of shimmering water as she let her arm fall to her side. People at the park were frozen in place as they were walking. Some were slightly reacting to the sound of the blast. Some looked as though they were just about to scream.

Esther went back to where John was standing and looked deeply into his eyes. *"This is like cheating,"* she thought to herself. *"He isn't looking into my eyes. Not really."* She was tempted to kiss him covertly, but felt that would be crossing a line somehow.

As Esther's curiosity got the best of her, she began looking around, searching for the origin of the blast. "There!"

She could see a shower of small particles of debris nearby. "These particles are moving!" she gasped. She carefully moved around the bits of metal fragments and small pieces of concrete and rock that were suspended in the air around her. They were moving… very, very slowly moving; only she seemed to be taken out of their time. Apparently, she was moving at a much faster rate!

"This is a new gift! I'll need to remember to discuss this with Mother!" she thought to herself.

As Esther began to calculate the trajectory of each particle, she became instantly alarmed. There, in front of her, was the Principal Chief of the Cherokee Nation—Bill John Baker—shaking hands with the Prime Minister of Israel, Benjamin Netanyahu! Surrounding them was a large group of children on a field trip of some sort. They each had a bright vest on for quick identification. The grenade appeared to have been tossed just in front of them!

Esther did a quick calculation in her mind. She estimated that there were probably about 38 fragments of flying metal and over 100 chunks of concrete in the air. The school group had 84 students and it looked like there were 6-8 adults with them as well. The dignitaries had about 6 body guards each, and there was a small camera crew.

She calculated that the danger area would be about 100 yards in diameter from the point of the explosion; but there were just about as many people in danger as there were particles in the area! It made more sense to gather the particles and do something else with them.

Because they were actually moving, their inertia would continue in the direction they were initially going. This made too many variables to control, but Esther had an idea. She could collect all of the fragments and place them in the nearby Delaware River.

One by one, Esther collected each small particle and bit of metal or concrete she could find. She placed them in a bag she found, as quickly as possible, starting from the center and working her way outward.

She finally finished gathering all of the pieces and threw them into the river. Then, she wondered how to get back into sync with time. That's when her mother's words came to her mind. *"Everything we hear is an opinion, not necessarily a fact. Everything we see is a perspective, not necessarily the truth."* That's it! She simply needed to change her "perspective" of time!

Esther closed her eyes, took a long deep breath, then she opened her eyes and focused her attention on the water droplets of the fountain before her. She zeroed in on the dance of the molecules, the surface tension that bounced portions of the sunlight into her eyes.

Suddenly, the water fountain began to move, and Esther found herself in the midst of a lot of confusion and a cloud of dust. She heard her name. John was frantically calling for her. "Here!" she shouted above the crowd. He was there in an instant. "How did you get over here so fast?" he yelled.

"Long story!" she replied, not sure if she should confide the rest of the story to her protector.

He quickly escorted her to where his motorbike was and they raced off to a quiet neighborhood where they could think, and talk. John began talking out loud to himself. "Sounded like an Mk2 World War II surplus pineapple grenade to me. Those things have a range of about 100 yards. We should have been hit! That's just weird! And the assassin should have taken cover somewhere about 30 yards from the point of impact, but I didn't see anyone…" His voice trailed off.

"And I didn't see you!" he said directly to Esther. "You were right next to me, and the next moment, you were on the other side of the Square!"

"I must be losing my mind!" he thought to himself as he slowly turned to Esther. *"Yup, I think I am losing my mind!"*

Esther began to think about people she noticed about 30 yards from the center of the explosion. She had been in and out of just about every inch of the area as she had been collecting small particles suspended in the air. No one seemed to stand out to her as the possible assassin. If she had thought of it before, she would have touched everyone in search for the culprit. The last 24 hours of that person's life would most certainly explain everything. Next time she would have to remember to do that.

"Next time?!" This thought jolted her back to the current moment.

Before she knew it, Esther was back at her hotel room. John had escorted her there without saying another word. They were both sort of numb and neither felt much like talking.

Chapter XVI

SMITHSONIAN'S NATIONAL ZOO

The next morning, Esther took the "T" transit to the Logan International Airport in East Boston. She wasn't paying much attention to people around her, and had tried to "turn off" the gift of 24-hour insight. It wasn't easy, but she found that she could do it if she prepared herself before touching a person. This was a tremendous help to her when being in contact with so many people on the local bus system, in a crowded street, or in a busy airport because it could get disorienting and exhausting.

Her next task was to try to control when she is able to see the auras of people. Up to this point, it just sort of happened when she didn't expect it. These two gifts will be especially helpful to her in her work with The Resistance.

As Esther thought about this, and relived the way she "stepped out of time," she wondered if she would be able to control this newest gift as well. Being totally absorbed in her own thoughts, she found herself focusing on two men near her who were sitting across from each other.

Their auras began to pulse with various shades of red and blue. An older man was wearing a New York Yankees baseball cap, while the younger man was wearing a Boston Red Sox cap. *"Well, that is inviting sparks!"* she thought to herself with a grin.

She could feel the tension in the small area intensify and the pulsing pattern of their auras ramped up exponentially. Suddenly, these two grown men were grabbing each other and wrestling with one another like a couple of toddlers throwing a tantrum.

Esther was not alarmed like everyone around her. She sat back and used the opportunity like a science experiment. She watched to see what colors and patterns their auras took as the grappled with one another. Interesting combinations and gyroscope designs manifested themselves with energy ribbons escaping in short bursts occasionally. It was really quite fascinating to watch. Who knows? This information might be helpful.

After her uneventful flight, Esther made her way to the Smithsonian's National Zoo where she was supposed to meet Robert. She looked around occasionally, and never noticed anyone following her.

This could mean that she really wasn't being followed. It could also tell her that she was all alone, and not being protected. Or, it could mean, that those following her are just that good.

Esther shrugged off those feelings and questions. It was 3:25pm. Robert should be there any moment now. She circled around, looking for any sign of him, but there was none. She tried not to be obvious about looking at her watch again.

A few minutes passed. No sign of him. Esther could feel the tension building in her body. *"Just relax! Breathe!"* she commanded herself.

She rehearsed his instructions to her. He said she was to meet him right here, near the entrance to the zoo, at 3:30pm on Saturday. *"Calm down…"* she instructed herself.

Each minute that passed felt like an unbearable mounting pressure. "Something must be wrong!" she whispered to herself.

As she scanned the scene around her, Esther turned on her ability to see auras. Most people have a creamy white aura unless they are sick or angry. Energy rises off of each person and bends the light around their frames, typically in a very even coating of glowing color that expands several inches just around the shapes of their bodies.

Occasionally, someone will have a very thick, bright, white aura that seems to have rays of light shining from them. Sometimes, there appears to be layers, like a layered cake, with narrow ribbons of color surrounding the person. These people usually seem to be hiding things about their character from the world.

One man, that Esther saw, seemed to have an extra ordinate amount of energy rising straight up from his head. Perhaps it was simply body heat rising off of his bald head! Or perhaps he was communicating with an extraordinary amount of mental thought. Whatever it was, she realized that she should ask her mother to help her understand what it all meant. After all, *"what good is having a spiritual gift if there is no purpose in it; if you can't help someone?"*

She checked her watch. It was 4:00pm. No Robert. Something definitely was wrong! She determined to return to her apartment, get something to eat, and then try to figure out what to do next.

As Esther gathered her bags and turned to head back out the entrance of the zoo, she noticed the aura of a solitary individual in the crowd. The woman seemed to be walking as if in a trance toward the administrative offices of the zoo. Her aura was throbbing like a pulsar with each step. Esther saw a glimpse of something strapped to her frame that looked like narrow cylinders in a row, a green flashing light, and some wires.

"Get down! It's a bomb!" she heard someone say before she realized that it had been her own voice.

As if in slow motion, she saw everyone around her start to crouch down and look around in terror. The woman with dark olive skin and black hair was wearing flowing robes that no longer covered her head. As their eyes met, Esther realized that she had never had anyone look at her with such hatred before. It startled her, and that was the moment she "stepped out" of time again.

She decided to touch the terrorist to see if she would be able to sense the last 24-hours of her life. It worked. This woman had been in a hospital room crying over the death of her only child just yesterday. Her despair was overwhelming. Esther could feel it all. The anguish almost brought her to her knees.

As she struggled to catch her breath and recover from the devastating feelings of hopeless despair, she looked into the eyes of the frozen woman before her again. This time, she felt compassion for her.

Esther reached around the statue figure before her to remove the bomb strapped to her waist and spoke from her heart. "All is not lost. Everything will be okay. You don't have to do this. You can go on. Continue, and you'll be fine. Keep breathing."

Esther did not know how to de-activate the bomb, so she decided to take it somewhere, where it wouldn't hurt anyone. All she could think of was the nearby pond in the park area. After throwing the package into the water, she checked around the perimeter to see if she needed to protect anyone else.

"All clear!"

Now, to re-enter the present time frame. Esther closed her eyes, relaxed her body, took a cleansing breath, and slowly opened her eyes to focus on the clouds floating unawares in the sky above her. She heard a loud BOOM nearby. The ground shook a little, and she smiled as she walked purposefully toward the exit gate to pick up her luggage and leave.

As she passed the Palestinian woman who was spinning around with an angry and confused look on her face. People were running around like ants after the entrance of their hill is disturbed.

Perhaps it was Esther's calm demeanor that made her stand out, or maybe it was their design to grab her anyway, but before she could make it to the exit gate, two armed men in black uniforms took hold of each arm and whispered to her that she should not make any sudden moves, and that she should go with them.

They were wearing rubber gloves, and she noticed that she couldn't sense the last 24 hours of their lives. This was new. Esther suddenly felt very vulnerable. She was used to feeling in control, having a secret edge. She did notice one thing – one very important detail. Each of the men had a SolMaize lapel pin. They didn't seem to be ashamed to wear them. This was something she would have to tell Robert about.

It was very difficult to explain why she wasn't running like everyone else, but eventually Esther was released to go home. Something didn't quite feel quite right, though. They didn't ask her enough questions. It felt as though they let her go too easily. Something was definitely suspicious about the entire thing.

After Esther left the room, Todd Bristol stepped out of an adjoining room. "I can't risk being seen by her for a while, not until we find out more about how involved she really is. Did you find the flash drive?"

"Nothing sir."

"That's alright. I have other options in my back pocket. Did you place the tracking dot on her purse?"

"As instructed, sir."

Esther suspected that they had gone through her luggage in the other room. It was a good thing she had hidden the flash drive inside her lipstick lid. All the way home, Esther went through her mind to think of what she should do, and what could have happened to Robert. *"I don't even know how to contact him!"* she thought exasperatedly.

As she entered her apartment, Esther quickly checked to see if there were any signs of forced entry. There didn't appear to be any. She took a quick inventory to see if anything were out of place. Good news, everything looked fine.

She plopped down heavily onto the bed, sighed deeply and closed her eyes. She had to figure out how to get in touch with Robert. She hoped he was alright. She needed to tell him about this newly discovered gift of stepping out of time. She had to tell him about Chloe, and John, and about the grenade, and the bomb… there was simply lots to tell him. With that, she drifted off into a restless sleep without ever getting undressed.

Chapter XVII

THE RESISTANCE

The next morning, Esther saw an envelope that had been slipped under her door. *"This is not the usual method. Can I trust this message?"* she thought to herself. On the back was a stamp. It was a circle with a large dash across it to cancel out or prohibit the image inside. Inside the circle was the sunflower and ear of corn image she had seen on that tie clip. "SolMaize" she whispered. Her eyes widened as she realized that is wasn't "SolMaize," but rather "The Resistance"—the organization fighting *against* SolMaize.

Esther, remembering the cameras in her apartment, pretended to straighten up her apartment by shuffling through her mail. After gathering a dishtowel and some cleanser, she took the arm load of supplies into the bathroom and closed the door.

The note looked like it was from Robert. He was letting her know that he was alright. He had heard about what had happened to her and wanted to make sure she was alright. "Meet me at the National Aquarium in the lower level of the Department of Commerce Building near the octopus exhibit today at 10am. Please make sure you are not followed. There have been some new developments."

Esther smiled to herself. She liked Robert. She liked it that he seemed to care about her – personally. Even though he was a little quirky, and his side-kick was sort of silly, she liked him. She liked him a lot. She didn't care about whatever "new developments" there were; she would get to see Robert again. The thought of that had her humming to herself as she got dressed and prepared to leave, making sure to bring the lipstick with the hidden flash drive in it, so she could hand the information over to Robert.

She made her way to the meeting place, carefully ensuring that she was not being followed. Then she spied John standing by the long-arched plastic tube with the octopus scrunched inside, moving through contortions as it made its way up the cylinder.

John was visibly relieved to see her. Somehow, this worried her a little bit. *"What's going on? I thought I was meeting Robert!"* she wondered anxiously. *"Where is Robert? Is he alright?"*

"I know you were probably expecting Robert," John said coyly. Esther looked at John. She had forgotten how cute his dimples were, and how intensely captivating his eyes were. "Uh, yes, er, I mean, um," she stammered.

Nodding toward the octopus, John asked, "Did you know octopi can use tools, walk on dry land, and are masters of intelligent escape?"

Stunned, Esther furrowed her brows, blinked her eyes a few times and shook her head. "What?"

John held her arms and looked intently into Esther's eyes. "You and I need to go immediately to the airport. I'm sorry, but we can't talk here. I'll tell you everything on the way." The flashes Esther saw as John touched her were confusing. She had so many questions, but she felt she could trust John implicitly.

As he rushed her into a taxi, Esther's head was spinning. Finally, she blurted, "John, wha…" and he swiftly put his finger on her lips to shush her. Without saying a word, he suddenly kissed her. At first, she was surprised, then she realized that she wasn't pulling away. She liked kissing John. *"Wait, I shouldn't just let him kiss me like this!"* she thought to herself as her mind sort of drifted off. Then she pulled back and looked surprisedly at him. Then, she felt her cheeks get hot as they blushed and she lowered her eyes in embarrassment. They both chuckled softly and were both quietly looking out their windows all the way to the airport.

"Not fair!" she blurted suddenly. "You're just trying to distract me from asking questions."

"Did it work?" he quipped.

She sighed, rolled her eyes, and turned to look out the window.

Esther felt as though she were in a daze all the way until they boarded the Boeing 767 American Airlines flight #11 that Monday morning. John made sure Esther was sitting near the window in the economy section, and he sat next to her in the aisle seat. Once everything settled down for the one hour and 16-minute flight, John turned to Esther and handed her a child's writing device. He had written a message on it. Once she had read it, he pushed a little button that cleared the screen and wrote another message for her to read. They silently did this the entire flight while John made sure to block the people behind them from seeing anything through the crack between the seats, and made sure to also block any view from across the isle as well.

He liked being close to Esther. He could smell her hair each time he bent closer to her. It smelled like Cinnamon Apples. He liked kissing her too, although he wasn't sure he should have. He didn't want to complicate things during a mission, and the feelings he was having could definitely complicate things!

Esther had a difficult time breathing. It wasn't because John was so close to her, but rather, it was the things she was reading that took her breath away.

"I am part of The Resistance too," he began. *"I am assigned to protect you. I volunteered. We learned that there is to be a terrorist attack in New York City sometime soon. It will be something that is designed to turn the world on its end. If it is to be stopped, at all, there is only one chance, and you are the key.*

"SolMaize has partnered with the Taliban and al-Qaeda because of common goals and interests. This has been in the works for a couple of years now. One thing about SolMaize is they are very patient, they have unlimited resources, and they always think globally. They also don't seem to have any boundaries or lines they won't cross to achieve their ultimate goals.

"The terrorist attack is meant to send a message to the United States that we are not safe from them, even in our own homes. It is meant to make a statement against capitalism and our free-market society. I believe New York City is their prime target because of the World Trade Center. You are key to our stopping this because of your special gifts."

Esther stopped and looked at John. This means that Robert told him that she had shared about when she touches someone. She suddenly didn't know how she felt about either of them! She certainly felt exposed, and she didn't like that one bit!

"I'm sorry if you feel betrayed by Robert telling me about that. We were discussing just how valuable you are to The Resistance right before he was taken."

At that, John looked into Esther's eyes, saying nothing, but trying to convey just how much he cared for her and never wanted to hurt her in any way. He tapped his index finger on his closed lips and slowly shook his head, then looked around the aircraft. She softened a bit and continued reading.

"We can save Robert, and possibly save many lives as well. There will be danger, but I will be with you the entire time. Are you in?"

"Now's a fine time to ask me that!" Esther thought to herself as she nodded. She couldn't wait for this day to end! Could it possibly get any worse?

Chapter XVIII

THE DAY BEFORE THE STORM

The day seemed normal for September in all other ways. It was typically hot, humid, and windy with grey storm clouds threatening to dump a quick inch of water on the unsuspecting 1.5 million people living in Manhattan. John explained that they were to go to the top of the Empire State Building to meet someone.

He took her hand as they pushed through the crowds and walked 10 blocks to the entrance of the iconic building. After riding the elevator to the 102nd floor, Esther and John stepped out to the observation deck after passing through the gift shop.

The wind was strong and made it difficult to hear each other, but the view was fantastic! A large white thunderhead was marching toward the Twin Towers with the south tower exhibiting 104 stories, making them some of the tallest buildings in the world.

A tall man, well over six feet, with steely eyes and yellow teeth wore a military uniform with lots of colorful ribbons and pins. There were four stars on his collar, so Esther knew he was a man of some importance. He explained that the Brigadier General placed him as Director of Operations at the Pentagon Command Center for tomorrow morning only. "It just doesn't smell right to me! I think it's going to happen tomorrow!" he shouted into the wind.

"I've had meetings cancelled with some of the top brass, and they won't say why. These are the same dirty snakes that I've been keeping an eye on for The Resistance! I tell you; something is up!"

Then, nodding toward Esther, he said, "This the one you were telling me about?" John nodded yes. "I don't see how she can help…"

John interrupted, and moving Esther towards the colonel, and winking at her, he said, "May I present miss Esther Cohen." They shook hands. As they did, the familiar 24-hour blast of pictures and information shot through Esther like a bolt of lightning. She tried to gain her composure, and John covered for her by distracting the colonel, then whisking Esther away.

Once they were alone, he turned to her. "Well?" Exasperated, she replied, "Where to begin! I don't know who you think he is, but he has accepted a large envelope of cash from an assistant to the Secretary of State, and I heard him say, 'Lowest parking level under the south tower.' He has made sure that a backup communications system is switched on to 'Exercise Mode' and ready for use. He was talking to someone about $2.3 trillion dollars missing from the Pentagon, and he called FEMA and told them to come to New York today. I can't tell which side he's on!"

John let out a long breath of relief. "I knew you would be the key!" he exclaimed, then he gave her an enthusiastic kiss on the lips and ran to the elevator – dragging her dazedly behind him by the hand.

The three-mile walk would have been a nice stroll except for the fact that they were almost running. Only the crowds and the street lights slowed their progress. Esther definitely did not wear the right shoes! She could feel a blister forming on her right heel as her shoe was rubbing against her bare skin. She was thirsty too, and starting to feel dizzy.

She started to see honeycomb shaped edges to her peripheral sight, and without warning, collapsed as they closed in on her. If John hadn't taken hold of her hand, he might not have seen her go down. But, because he did have her hand, he was able to catch her. Holding her in his arms was nice… but he had to wake her! "Please wake up!" He shook her gently at first, then more vigorously. "Esther, please wake up! You have to be alright!"

As Esther slowly came to, she blinked her eyes a few times, then realized she was lying on the concrete and in John's arms. Although she was quite comfortable there, looking into his hazel eyes, this wasn't the time nor the place! She started to get up, and was pleased at the way John helped her. It sort of felt like dancing.

She needed to get something to eat and drink. Her blood sugar was too low. A street vendor was selling hot dogs nearby. As they approached the cart, they looked at each other – remembering how they met – and burst out laughing. But the cool water they bought did help her feel better; not so weak and dehydrated. They would find something else to eat along the way; anything but a hot dog!

Eventually, John led Esther to the 2nd tower of the World Trade Center. Carefully checking to make sure they were not followed, they used the stairs to enter the lowest parking level of the South Tower.

John quietly motioned for Esther to stay back as he pulled out his Glock 17 and quickly checked to make sure it was loaded. Esther held her breath and stood with her back against the wall while John went ahead, looking around each pillar in swift stealthy movements, in each closet, and inspecting each potential hiding place. At each turn, he would motion for her to join him.

Finally, they came to a locked door with a motion detector affixed to the top. John took Esther's hand and placed it on the door. "Can you feel anything?" he asked earnestly.

Esther desperately wanted to sense something. She tried to extend her awareness into the adjoining room, but something was blocking her. She strained to expand her senses, she closed her eyes, took a deep breath, and focused on the molecules of the door beneath her hand. She could sense their energy and movement. Slowly, she mentally made her way into the locked room, and there he was!

Esther gasped, "It's Robert! He's in there!" she whispered. "How can we get him out? He's tied to a chair, and there is someone else in there with a rifle!"

"Leave that to me!" John said as he dug deep into his pants pocket to retrieve a multi-purpose pocket knife. He carefully used the Phillips screw driver to remove the casing, then gently detached the battery. That's all it took. John kicked in the door and in one smooth motion rushed the armed guard, knocked him unconscious, and freed Robert by cutting the plastic zip ties that bound him.

It all happened so fast that Esther scarcely had time to process what was occurring. Robert had been beaten. He was filthy and weak, and required assistance to get out of the chair.

Draping his arms over each of their shoulders, Esther and John helped Robert to a bathroom on the main floor of a nearby building, and locked the door. As they did, Esther relived the last 24 hours of torture, taunting, deprivation, and misery Robert had experienced. She also knew that he had been thinking about her to get himself through it all and to survive each day. Esther got a drink of water for him from the sink, her heart filled with compassion for the man.

Robert told them that a brigadier general had been questioning him about what he knew about money missing from the Pentagon; about a top-secret message to the NASDQ and a warning bell; and also about stock market options. None of it seemed to make sense.

Suddenly Esther remembered the flash drive she was supposed to deliver to Robert at the Smithsonian's National Zoo a few days ago. She reached into her pocket and pulled out the miniature flash drive and placed it into Robert's hand. As their hands touched, she felt a tingling sensation and a chill fill her body. She blushed, looked down, then looked up at John who was watching her intently.

As though she were changing the subject, Esther started to unlock the door and gather things saying, "I think we need to get Robert out of here."

Chapter XIX

TIME IS THE FIRE IN WHICH WE BURN

That evening, Esther relaxed on the hotel bed, lying on her back and going over the events of the day. She was disturbed by the potential terrorist attack, and worried about how Robert was feeling. He was being held in a top security hospital ward, so she couldn't be with him, but she knew he was in good hands.

She found herself analyzing how she felt about Robert and how she felt about John. There were several similarities between the two of them. She felt herself going back and forth between them in her affections. This cannot continue. A decision will need to be made, but how to choose between them?

She pulled out her Bloodwood Flute and stroked its smooth barrel. She rolled it around slowly under the light, appreciating the golden shimmering grain of the wood. After taking a slow deep breath, she closed her eyes and put the flute to her lips.

The mellow tones of the Native American flute filled the room and instantly created a resonating chamber like the Church of Saint Anne in

Jerusalem. Each note seemed to hang in the air for a full three seconds until it dissipated. It left Esther with the effect of playing a duet with herself. The timbre of her flute had a reverberation that seemed to transport the entire room with it to the heavens. It always felt surreal when Esther played her mother's flute.

As expected, Ziven appeared to her daughter, only this time Esther wasn't smiling. "Mother," Esther began, "I'm not sure what is going to happen, or what my part in it should be." She continued, "I feel that something bad is about to happen; something big. I recognize that I am here in this place at this time for a purpose. I don't want to mess up. I'm fearful of making a mistake. Lives could be at stake."

Ziven lifted her hand, which silenced Esther immediately. Then, she gave her daughter a compassionate smile. "My dear, a poet named Delmore Schwartz once said 'Time is the fire in which we burn.' I would add that it is fleeting, and full of hot emotion. Our people were called The People of the Fire anciently; that's what Cherokee literally means. And, if you remember, we were also called Ana Shina'Abe, or the People of Shinar. Shinar was the mountain at the place where the people settled after the baptism of the earth in ancient days. It is the place near where the tall ziggurats were built as all the people and on the face of the land became wicked. It is where our people fled from after the confounding of the languages when our people were retained as a whole due to the faithful prayers of our Blessed Fathers."

Esther looked at her mother, waiting intently for the message she was trying to explain. "Mother Earth must now undergo another baptism. Not of water, but of fire. My child, our people represent the place where there will be a gathering after this second baptism. We will rise up as The Ana Shina'Abe again! You will save not only our people, but all of humanity! It is your destiny."

Esther felt overwhelmed. How could *she* save humanity? "But how, Mother?" Ziven smiled, "You will know. You will feel it and be inspired as to what to do. I, and others, will be with you. Everything will be alright. Have faith!" And with that, Ziven faded away.

Esther found herself lying on her back on the hotel bed. The room seemed dark and much smaller. "I don't know, Mother," she whispered, shaking her head and breathing out a long sigh. "I just don't know."

The next morning, Esther awoke with a start. The hair on the back of her neck raised. She threw on some clothes and went out onto the balcony of the hotel room which overlooked the murky Hudson. She couldn't greet the sun like she wanted to, but she performed her morning ritual of greeting the new day with the promise that she would "serve The Creator with all her heart, might, mind, and strength all the days of her life" as her mother had taught her was the tradition of the Cherokee People from ancient times.

She couldn't relax though. There was an eerie feeling in the air. She couldn't put her finger on it. She had received a message that Robert would be released from the hospital today, but he had to still be quite weak from his ordeal. She only knew that she needed to see him. It was an urgent feeling she couldn't shake.

A stench from red tide was in the air. September mornings were unpredictable but there was not much wind, and the sky was cloudless and clear. From her window she could hear the usual sounds of a city with over eight million residents and over 40 million tourists visiting the city each year.

It was 8:30 in the morning. The bustling of businesses opening, people filling the streets, cars honking impatiently in bumper-to-bumper traffic, and excited school groups touring historic sites created quite a commotion that seemed to rise off of the concrete jungle like the fog of San Francisco as it lifts—fluid, connected, and unstoppable.

8:48am

Then she saw it.

A commercial jet, much like the one she had just flown in on yesterday, was flying far too low. It looked like it was going to fly right between the two towers of the World Trade Center! Esther blinked her eyes and shook her head. Was she really seeing this happen or was she imagining it?!

Esther gasped as she watched the 767-jet plow right into the tower! Eyes blinking back tears, she was stunned and didn't realize she was holding her breath. Her mouth opened as she surveyed the surreal scene. An explosion, fire, and billowing smoke poured out like dry ice fumes flowing out of the newly-formed hole in the obelisk to capitalism. She could see large pieces of debris floating and falling down in slow motion, and continued fire at the jagged edges of what used to be the beautiful New York landscape and the symbol of prosperity.

Sirens began heading toward the towers as the fire department rushed toward the horrific scene. Esther just stood there, motionless, in disbelief and shock at the sight. *"So, this is what Robert and John were talking about!"*

With that thought, Esther jerked herself into reality and tried to call the front desk to get the room numbers for John and Robert. She felt so stupid that she hadn't any other way to contact them. She rushed down to the lobby, but no one was there. There were people outside near the front doors pointing up at the sky.

9:03am

Esther joined them only to look up and watch helplessly as a second plane hit the other tower of the World Trade Center! *"What is happening! Is this real?!"*

People began running in the streets as mass hysteria took over. Confetti filled the air like a ticker-tape parade. Business women and men were running through littered streets carrying whatever they could. Esther stood in the middle of the street with thousands of others, covering her mouth, wiping her tears, and trying to make sense of what she was witnessing. Time stood still, or did it?

9:05am

The two towers looked like chimneys with a large trail of grey smoke streaking the clear sky. Huge flames in the center of the buildings could be seen for miles. Mangled steel looked like jagged teeth in the mouth of a creature as the gaping hole sucked in the smoke from the other building.

9:08am

"No!" Esther heard herself cry out as she saw people jumping from the 78th floor to get away from the flames! Firefighters were sent up, but the policemen on the ground sobbed in helpless disbelief of what they were seeing, and their inability to stop it.

9:13am

79th street in Manhattan was engulfed in flames. JFK and LaGuardia's airports stopped all incoming traffic. Times Square displayed the horrific scene on the GMA billboard. Mothers held their children close, men wiped their tears, and Esther was a statue. A statue with tears streaming steadily down her ash-covered cheeks.

9:16am

Police had large pieces of metal placed in the middle of the street as they geared up with helmets and shields, preparing for riot control. All of the surrounding buildings were evacuated, but word was that people were stuck in some of the elevators.

"I heard someone say that a plane would hit something every half hour!" she heard someone behind her say. Not wanting to believe it, Esther shook her head quickly as though doing so would fling the terrifying thought out of her mind.

9:21am

The streets for eight miles in every direction were covered with ash. Burning embers and papers were on fire as firefighters prepared to go into the smoldering tinderboxes carrying tanks of oxygen and looking much like gladiators entering an arena to face their own mortality. Medics carried people to ambulances and were trying to keep order. Cell phone towers were not able to carry the volume, of course, and a cascaded failure made them stop working at all. Panicked people were stuck on Ellis Island, in subways, and in elevators.

The sounds of every-day urban life were instantly replaced by a profoundly shocked silence which at once included an underlying hysteria, panic, and tears. Those on the street walked in stunned silence like they were sleepwalking in a nightmare they couldn't awaken from.

Waves of people from all walks of life poured out of the subways and tall buildings onto the streets like a plague of ants rising up from the bowels of the earth. They flowed out onto the surface and had to keep moving to make room for the masses continuing to push their way up and out.

At Times Square, the President's face was larger than life on the huge monitor as he asked Americans to pause for a moment of silence. Even the agnostic respectfully paused, for this horrendous event had taken place on American soil! We'd been attacked in our own home!

9:35am

In the windows above the fire that was clinging to the twisted steel and open wounds in the great pillars, were people hanging outside to get away from the blazing smoke, waving flags and clothing in a desperate plea for rescue.

The fireman on the walkie-talkie near Esther was saying, "Stay where you are! Remain low to the ground and remain calm. We're doing the best we can. We're in the building and will get to you as soon as possible. Sit tight. Stay where you are. Break a window and wait for us to lead you out of there. Don't leave your floor!" Then he released the button and put his hand on his forehead in disbelief, shaking his head.

Esther surveyed the devastation. Fruit stands were abandoned at the farmer's market, ashes covered buildings and cars as though a volcanic explosion had kicked up a ton of ash and spewed it out to cover the entire surface of the earth. The shocked faces of every person were also covered with a thick layer of ash, streaked with tears. In all other ways, it was like a ghost town.

9:42am

Thousands of people were silently walking uptown, away from the horror. Silently, that is, except for the sniffing, coughing, and sighs. The smell of Red Tide was easily drowned out with the smell of burning wire and metal. Esther didn't join the flow of bodies. She had to stay put to find John and Robert. "Where are they?!" she said exasperatedly as she began to pace back and forth.

Someone walking by said they had heard that another plane had crashed into the Pentagon. *"How could this be happening?!"* Esther screamed silently, the tension building up inside of her like a pressure cooker.

9:54am

Flames in the buildings became more intense. Esther heard the Fire

Chief say that the inside walls of the tower were breached. The voice on his walkie-talkie said that the elevator is messed up, and that there were injured people on the 70th floor. The voice started to sound panicked as it said, "We need to get to the elevators past the 40th floor! There is a lot of smoldering debris." The Chief said, "We see two isolated pockets of fire from here, and there are people above you hanging out of their windows." The voice answered desperately, "Right! We're on the 77th floor now, but can't get past the 78th floor unless we get some more water up here, right now!"

9:59am

At that instant, like right out of a nightmare, the structure before her imploded and collapsed! A billowing flaming cloud of smoke invaded between the buildings, clamoring for space. People began running to beat the pyroclastic cloud, but of course, it caught up with them, overpowering them as though a nuclear bomb went off in their midst. A fine dust thickly covered people, permeating their hair, their eyes, ears, noses, and mouths, everything! Visibility was zero. Then the hot smoke turned darker as it rushed past, full of bricks, glass, concrete, pieces of metal, and pieces of people!

Esther didn't run. Her feet felt as though they were rooted deep into the ground. She closed her eyes and covered her face with her shirt, but she could hear people screaming and crying out as they were being hit by debris and choking in the blackness of the ash and dust. Their cries seemed to be even louder than all of the smoke alarms going off in the surrounding buildings, the police and fire engine sirens and horns, and even louder than the sound of the explosion itself.

That was it! She couldn't take it anymore! She had to force herself to step out of this time! She had to help as many people as she could!

Suddenly, everything got deathly quiet. Esther uncovered her face and slowly opened her eyes afraid of what she might see. Was the horror over? No. She had just successfully stepped out of this time.

Even the particles of ash were still, hanging in the air. As she moved her hand, she left a trail of openness in the air. Distracted momentarily by the illogical nature of the situation, she made a smiley face in the dust. Then, being overcome with emotion because of the seriousness of the moment, she wiped it away and quickly made her way toward the remaining tower.

As Ester walked due west, towards the tower, she could only see about a foot in front of her. Each time she found someone about to be hit by something, she would move the item, or knock the person down so they will not be touched. She could see that the particles were moving, but very slowly to her point of view.

She made her way up the remaining tower and saw firefighters trying to call loved ones to say they are alright. They were wearing face masks and gearing up with crowbars, shovels, oxygen tanks, hoses, etc. She saw people bloody and wounded, helping others to escape. As she made her way up one of the main stairwells, she could feel the heat of the flames, even though they were almost still.

Checking each floor, she made her way up the building, helping to ensure that people she could help were saved, but her heart was breaking. There was not much she could do! Even with time being halted to a snail's pace, there were too many people, and she couldn't save them! She couldn't save them!!

Then she heard it! A crashing sound in the silent stillness! Her feet felt uneasy beneath her. A thought came to her like a whisper, *"Get out now! This building is falling too!"*

As though in slow motion herself, she started to run toward the stairwell, but the floor beneath her feet started to lower with each step. She never made it to the stairwell, and she noticed that the twisted steel and concrete were speeding towards her as she began to fall. It was as though she were literally falling into time.

10:28am

The second tower, the north one, also imploded as the world breathlessly watched in horror. It sent more ash, debris, and smoke surging and sending people running yet again, like a nebulous monster reaching for and catching anyone who dares to run away.

The entire of Manhattan was totally engulfed in billowing clouds of smoke, dust, and ash. Children were frightened, and scared even more by their parent's panic. Surely the world could never be the same.

Chapter XX

WAR ZONE

10:35am

Large pieces of smoldering debris floated in the air like snowflakes. The scene was surreal and everyone seemed to be in shock. Robert, on the other hand, was frantic! People around him were covered with fine dust and walking, walking, walking like refugees away from the center of the free world. He was covered with dust too, but heading the other direction. He had to find Esther!

Robert's ribs were wrapped, his right arm was in a sling, and he had several bandages and stitches all over his body. But with all of the ash and devastation… he didn't seem to stand out at all.

"Oh, dear God!" He cried. "What have I done? She's all alone, and …" he bowed his head in shame. "How am I ever going to find her!" he exclaimed. *"That is, IF she's still…"* Unable to finish the thought, and unwilling to entertain it at all, he forged forward. On toward the skeletal, ragged remains of two of the tallest buildings in the world.

Calling out as he walked on what seemed to be a dusty planet in a science fiction movie, Robert trudged onward. *"Why did I have to meet with The Resistance this morning to deliver the flash drive of information Esther had given me? Why didn't I let Esther know where I was? What if she… How could I ever survive without her? Maybe John would be there to protect her. That's it, John is probably with her right now."* Robert's step slowed slightly.

"John is probably comforting her right now…" With that, Robert's countenance changed and his step increased to a slight jog again.

His lungs were burning and he was coughing violently. He couldn't catch his breath. His ribs were hurting with each spasm. There didn't seem to be enough oxygen in the world to keep him from passing out, but he had to keep going! He had to be sure she was safe! He had to find Esther!

As Robert was making his way through the burned-up vehicles and twisted steel, angry survivors began fighting each other sending up dust clouds as they hit each other in desperate, yet impotent rage.

Robert stopped near where the World Trade Center used to be, stunned at the sight. Blinking tears away at the tremendous loss, he took a deep breath, which started a coughing spell from the depths of his lungs, and blood along with the blackened mucus. *"No time to think about that now. I've got to find Esther!"*

Windows of all the buildings he could see were blown out. Everything was the same shade of grey. Everything that is except for the bloody handprints that lined the few remaining walls.

Robert found a dirty sink. He turned the x-shaped knob counter-clockwise, and fresh water slowly began washing away the thick layer of silt from the sink's porcelain bowl. Robert began cleansing his hands and face. Suddenly his hands were red with blood; his blood! He did a quick assessment. The side of his head was bleeding. *"Headwounds always bleed too much,"* he thought to himself. *"No worries. I just need to find Esther!"*

At that, he knelt down, holding onto the porcelain sink for stability. "Dear Father! I don't know where to look. I have no idea where to even begin. Please! Please guide me and direct me, that I may find Esther! I know that I have not been perfect in Thy sight, yet, I humbly come before Thee and ask Thee to use me as an instrument in Thy hands to bring this favored daughter of Thine to safety! Please, Father! Tell me where to go. Tell me where to look. Help me, please! In the name of Jesus, I beg Thee to help me in this, my hour of need! Amen."

At that, he took a deep breath and listened. He listened with every molecule of his soul. Then, like a beautiful spring day, a thought came into his mind. He could see Esther lying unconscious inside some sort of dark box. She was hurt, but she was breathing.

Robert walked purposefully as he "felt" the direction he should go. Climbing over concrete and steel rubble, climbing over the remains of vehicles, busses, and even the dead, he pushed forward for what felt like an eternity. Searching. Sensing. Searching.

Climbing over a chunk of steel, his thoughts were drawn to dig straight down at that very spot, but how? How could he move tons of concrete and steel? He was going to need to get some help, and soon!

Chapter XXI

AIRFORCE ONE

6:30am

Earlier that morning, John had to attend a CIA briefing. Nothing unusual, but the hair on his neck rose as they closed the meeting. He was to fly on Airforce One with the President of the United States for a "sleeper of a trip" to Florida. The President would visit an elementary school and talk about education. *"I've got a bad feeling about this,"* he said to himself.

With heightened awareness, he helped guard the Commander in Chief. Yet, at the same time, he found his thoughts wandering to a certain ginger he knew. His mind would meander briefly, a slight smile would cross his lips, and then he would draw himself back to the task at hand.

8:46am

As the President was preparing to visit with the elementary school children, John heard in his earpiece, "A commercial jet has crashed into one of the Twin Towers. CIA is scrambling to determine if it is a terrorist action, but facts are unknown at this time."

The Chief of Staff informed the President, but he thought the pilot of the downed plane must have had a heart attack or something. "Let's continue as planned," was his instruction.

9:03am

John heard a frantic voice in his earpiece. "A 2nd airplane has hit the other tower! America is under attack!" He watched surreally as the Chief of Staff made the decision to interrupt the President, who was enjoying reading to the classroom of elementary school children. He whispered in the President's ear, then stepped away.

So, this was the catastrophic strike Bin Laden's informers were hearing about! Up to this point, nothing had been actionable. Well, that just changed! The media and staff room had obviously just learned the horrifying news as well, and waited breathlessly for the President's response, but what could be done and said in front of these small children?

The President stared off into space for about five seconds. The Press tried to ask him questions, but he motioned to them to wait to talk about it later. Then, he waited for an opportune moment to exit without causing distress to the young children. "Mr. President, you are not safe here. It's been televised live that you are here!" John urged. "The american people need to hear from me," he answered resolutely.

After a brief statement, a few questions, and a moment of silence, the motorcade rushed at breakneck speed to get to the aircraft as soon as possible. The engines were already running because Security knew that Airforce One was a sitting duck. "Move it! Move it!" John shouted as the President and his party boarded.

Everyone on board had to hold on tightly as the jet began taxying down the runway and then turned abruptly because someone with a "long gun" was at one end of the runway. The takeoff was at a 45-degree angle. It was so steep that it was almost dizzying for the President's staff.

It wasn't difficult for John, though. His Explosive Ordinance Disposal training in the Marines was far worse than this. He remembered the day he was learning to detect explosive devices on the bottom of an Aircraft Carrier; swimming in shallow areas with inches between his chest and the ocean floor. There was the time he was learning to sky dive in the dark into enemy territory. Then, there was the POW training; learning how to withstand torture and capture... but he didn't want to think about that now. He had to bring himself back to the task at hand; back to Angel Flight.

John heard the pilot say that they only had four hours of fuel. There was no communication with the ground, so of course no one on the ground knew who was in command. "Probably mass hysteria down there," John whispered to the other body guard.

He looked over at the President. In the few times he had been called to protect this man, he had grown to admire his intellect and moral character. The president prior to this one could speak to the masses comfortably, as long as his speech was prepared in advance. He seemed to view himself much like a rock star in public. But in private, he was a totally different person. He'd spend a lot of time playing video games and smoking (a thing he told the American people he had stopped doing), but he could barely put two intelligent sentences together on his own.

But this president was an enigma. Private one-on-one conversations were very thought-provoking and deep, yet when he got in front of the camera, he stammered and seemed ill-at-ease. Perhaps that is what endeared John to the man. And now, this situation required real leadership. John had every confidence that the President would make the best decisions possible because he surrounded himself with brilliant leaders that he listened to and respected.

9:45am

John saw the mantle of the Commander in Chief weigh heavily on the President as he said, "We're at war," to his aids. He became irritated and angry that the pilot would not take him to Washington, D.C. "But, sir, our job is to keep you safe!" John protested. The pilot added, "We must follow established protocols to protect you, sir!" The President fumed at the pilot, "It's not your call!" he shouted.

10:10am

Airforce One, or "Angel Flight", turned away from returning to Washington. It travelled alone, with no fighter support. John overheard the pilot say that he had called in for a "fighter bubble" but that it would be one hour before they could be protected because of post-Cold War military cutbacks of all things!

This flying "Whitehouse" was larger than the one on the ground! It was 230 feet long, had a 195 foot wing span, and was 6 stories tall. This 747-200 aircraft had been gutted and remodeled with a presidential apartment and office, walls with lamps that were nailed down, muted colors for comfort, a hospital section in case they had to do surgery, living room area with sofa, big comfortable 1st class seats, a conference room, 19 televisions, 38 telephones, multiple stations in the radio office, and many other luxuries. It was quite a sight.

John turned to the Chief of Staff and said, "Sir, I recommend we go to extreme security mode." He agreed, so John and several other Secret Service personnel searched the aircraft. An armed officer was posted at the stairwell from the base to the front of the plane. If there was a threat on board, they had done all they could.

Airforce One had no capability for offense, and only a few counter measures as defense against possible threats in the air. The Chief of Staff and pilot decided to fly higher than usual to avoid any regular traffic. This way, they could assume that anything flying 15,000 feet higher than regular airliners would be on an attack level. The unfortunate side effect was that radio contact with the ground was sketchy because of the height. This also disconnected them from everything happening on the ground.

10:40am

John noticed that tensions and appropriate paranoia were mounting onboard. He could feel it too. It had been one hour since takeoff, two hours since the attack began, they were still flying unprotected, and their destination was unclear. *"How am I supposed to protect the President? How am I supposed to protect Esther? Oh Esther! I hope Robert is there, taking care of you! Well, I'm not exactly sure how I feel about that, but as long as you are being taken care of..."* and his mind replayed the two times he kissed her... over and over.

Eventually, in the Press cabin toward the rear of the plane, there was a Press television that would flicker on and off with glimpses of what was happening below. People on the ground were knit together, but Airforce One was far removed.

The FAA and NORAD communication systems were incompatible, so the military didn't know where to send the fighters. Frustrations onboard Airforce One continued to mount.

11:24am

The radio crackled to life with a warning that two unidentified airplanes were on their tail! "Mr. President, brace for attack!" John shouted. Tears were streaking down the faces of the President's aids, "This is it!" one of them cried as she put her head down and sobbed.

John had no time to panic. He had to make sure the President was safe. *"Honor above all!"* He would have to worry about Esther later.

Suddenly, the pilots were laughing! They shouted, "F-16s, our Texas cover has just arrived!" An immediate sense of relief filled the cabin. Everyone released their emotions with laughter, tears, and some closed their eyes and sent gratitude heavenward. Now, with two heat-seeking missiles, and a hot gun each, if this incident takes a turn in any direction, they were prepared for anything!

This meant that they could lower their altitude and establish communications. They learned that the pentagon had been hit by an airplane! A sense of despair gripped the occupants of the President's plane. John could feel it in the air like a thick, dark, coldness that could never be comforted.

The phone rang. It was the Pentagon. "Another inbound airplane, highjacked, 16 miles south of Pittsburg, is heading toward Washington, D.C. at a high rate of speed. Permission to take it out?"

The President, without hesitation, stated, "You are weapons free!" Then he turned to his staff and said, "I was a fighter jet pilot, and I can't imagine getting orders like that." From that moment on, any commercial airplane with its transponder turned off, faces being immediately shot down. "Our world will never be the same," John muttered under his breath.

Moments later the radios were busy. A plane was down in Pennsylvania. Had the United States just shot down a commercial jet? It was unclear.

Black smoke filled the screens of the televisions. United flight #93 was down. There were no survivors. Everyone onboard was intently watching the newscast in stunned silence. Someone whispered out loud what no one would want to actually ask, "Did we shoot that plane down?"

The thought instantly struck every individual in the plane with the same profound sadness. No one breathed. 30 seconds later, the news came, "Not shot down! Just crashed!"

A flood of relief swept over everyone again! Only this time, it was a combination of elation and despair. The roller-coaster ride of emotions was beginning to take its toll.

The President called John over and said, "I need to talk to the American people! They need to know that I am alright!" "Mr. President…" John stated, shaking his head. He continued to try to persuade John to get him on the ground. "The first job of the President is to protect the nation. The second job is to talk to the country to give them a sense of purpose and direction. We need to land as soon as possible! Can you get me onto the ground?" John sighed deeply and promised, "I'll do what I can, Mr. President." "Thanks!" the President said with a pat on John's shoulder.

John convinced the Chief of Staff and the pilot to land at Barksdale Airforce Base in Treeport, LA. They have a massive fleet of bombers and were only 15 minutes away. Preparations were made to fuel Airforce One with 150 thousand pounds of gas, 70 box lunches, 25 pounds of bananas, 4 gallons of juice and coffee! They called it "Code Alpha."

11:45am

Airforce One landed, but as luck would have it, the base was in lock down because they were doing some sort of drill. B-52s were lined up with their pilots in their seats. They were preparing for a war game. Nuclear weapons were sitting side-by-side with the President's plane! "We are very vulnerable here, Mr. President!" John protested. "I need to speak to the American people! I need to let them know that the presidency and our nation are resolved to pass this test. I'll just make a quick statement, and we'll be on our way."

John didn't breathe easily until they were back up in the air. At this point, the President was left alone with his thoughts. John could see that they weighed terribly on him. This burden is a very lonely burden. John felt compassion for the man.

The news came in that every plane in the sky across the entire United States was ordered to land. "That'll cost the FAA billions of dollars!" someone said. "I don't care about their billions! The safety of the American people comes first!" the President snapped. Everyone was quiet after that, and kept their opinions to themselves.

2:00pm

The skies were not safe enough for the President to return to Washington, so he went to New York to see the towers. It had been over five hours since the attack began. Airforce One flew to the military facility there as part of the National Response Plan. A make-shift motorcade was created to whisk the President and his staff to a small cinder-block square building with stairs leading down, down, down, to the Command Center through a fire escape. It was like a rabbit hole. Only a skeleton staff was allowed into the underground bunker.

Finally, the President was able to talk to his security team. John was left to guard the entrance until his relief came. After that, he was free to leave. Dutifully he waited, but as he waited his impatience grew, and his thoughts were filled with… Esther.

Chapter XXII

OUT OF DARKNESS

Esther tried to open her eyes. She thought they were open, but she could not see anything. *"Am I blind?"* she thought anxiously. Her head was exploding and her eyes were burning. She felt weak. She couldn't seem to catch a breath. Her throat was dry. It was so dry that she couldn't force it to swallow.

She felt smooth walls and seemed to be in some sort of box or something similar with smooth walls. She quickly inventoried her body. Everything hurt, but something was wrong with her leg. She reached down to her left knee, but as she slid her hand down toward her ankle, the flesh where her shin bone should have been was soft. *"That can't be good!"* she thought. "Grea… Great!" she managed to say.

"It doesn't hurt, though! That's probably my brain protecting me because it would be too much to bear," she reasoned. Dizziness overtook her senses, and she lost consciousness again.

At that moment Robert felt a wave of urgency sweep over him. "We've got to hurry! She's down there! We haven't much time left!" he shouted at the driver of the hydraulic excavator he managed to direct to the spot where he "felt" Esther would be.

Robert shouted silent prayers heavenward, *"Please, dear God! If this is the right spot, please let her be alright!"*

There was no other reason why she should be there. He was fully trusting in the "feelings" of his heart. Robert had learned to trust these feelings long ago, but never had someone else's life depended upon him getting the still and small promptings absolutely correct. To say he was nervous would be a huge understatement. And his cough was getting worse.

The instant his relief arrived, John began to make his way from the "Rabbit Hole" toward the World Trade Center, or rather, where it used to be. It had been six hours since this whole nightmare began. Surely Esther was safe somewhere. Safe with Robert! That thought steamed John more than he cared to admit. He had been trying to avoid that image in his mind ever since this whole thing started.

He tried his cell phone again, but no service. The towers are either down, or their circuits are overloaded. He'd just try again later. *"Texts can sometimes get through when service is spotty,"* a thought entered his mind. So, he sent a text for Esther to call him, but as he continued block after block, his concern for her safety swelled into frantic desperation, and he picked up the pace.

The sky was blue, but everything else he could see was ash-grey. It was as though someone came and drained all of the color from the world. People's faces, their hair, clothing, everything (even the air) was covered with ash. The road, it seemed to be a road, was covered with several inches of fine soot and littered with books, papers, pieces of furniture, ragged chunks of concrete, and occasionally poking up were black twisted metal pieces. It was like something out of the movie, The War of the Worlds!

John didn't realize that he stood out until a child pointed out that he wasn't covered in ash like everyone else was. His panic began to rise with each step as he saw more and more sorrowful and sobbing people. Any one of them could be Esther! "How am I going to ever find her?!" he sighed exasperatedly.

It was then that Robert saw him coming. His dark suit and tie made John stand out in stark contrast. "John! Over here!" he shouted, coughing at the strain.

John looked up and picked up the pace to where Robert, ignoring his arm sling, was shoveling dirt and rubble away with his bare hands frantically as the excavator would remove large pieces of debris.

John's eyes were wild with fear at what this meant. "Esther?" he managed. Robert pointed to the hole that was being created. "She's down there!"

"What happened?"

Robert didn't know. Also, he wasn't sure what John's beliefs were, and knew he didn't have time to get into a philosophical discussion about spiritual matters. There was only time to save Esther!

"We can talk about that later! Dig!" he snapped.

Chapter XXIII

THE GREAT DISCOVERY

Esther was in a dark place, maybe it was a cave, she wasn't sure. She saw a pinpoint of light in the distance. She felt irresistibly drawn to it. Something was pulling her toward it and she seemed to have no choice.

As the light became larger and brighter, she noticed that it appeared that she was in some sort of tunnel. She didn't feel cold or hot. In fact, she didn't feel anything! Nothing was solid beneath her, and there was no sensation of a physical nature at all. Weird!

There was something she felt inside, though. It was like a warm, sparkling tremor in her chest that filled her with sweet happiness. This quickly grew to become a joyful feeling that swelled inside of her and past the perimeter where she felt her body was.

At that moment, she could see a lot of flowers near her feet. They were flowers of every type and color imaginable. In Esther's study of microbiology and genetics, there are just some colors that cannot be created, yet there they were – right before her very eyes! She tried to see between the molecules of these beautiful creations – to analyze their elements – but the moment she tried to do so she was tremendously distracted by what she heard!

Well, she didn't exactly "hear" it. It was more like she "felt" it. Their song was more vibrant and glorious than the songs of plants and elements she had heard before. Their voices were beautifully clear and pitched into harmonies she had never imagined. They were singing praise to The Creator. They were giving thanks and singing praise!

Instantly, she noticed a babbling brook near the flowers with a small bridge arching over it. The bridge was small, but elegant, and connected to a pathway. She couldn't tell what it was made of, perhaps some sort of stone.

As Esther's eyes followed the pathway into the distance, she became aware of a magnificent city of light! It was glowing and shot beams of energy into a night's sky. Somewhere in that city she could sense beings joining with elements of energy, intellect, light, and love, in singing songs of praise and gratitude. It was as though the entire city were in perfect harmony. A combining of unity of purpose without any reservations whatsoever.

Esther looked down again at the nearby water and smiled. She had heard the sparkling sounds of water singing praise before, but this was exquisite! The happy, shimmering waves picked up the colors of the nearby flowers and passed them along in sparkling and stunning rainbow colors that would flit and flicker. Their song was delicious to Esther's soul. She felt such love and peace fill her very being. She felt content to remain there forever and just…"feel."

Looking back up at the city of light, Esther suddenly realized that someone was approaching her. She didn't know who it was, but she didn't feel frightened; in fact, she felt a soothing wave of peace wash over her. She felt profoundly loved without any reservations.

As the Being crossed the bridge to the side Esther was on, He spoke her name, "Esther." It was as though electricity shot through her and then off into space, for as He said that one word, He spoke volumes! Communicated to her mind were layers upon layers of love and understanding. Her name meant the very essence of who she was and who she would become. It meant all of her thoughts, feelings, and experiences. It meant all of her hopes and dreams, her spiritual gifts, and her purpose in life. Her name – when He spoke it – meant all of these things!

He reached out His hand. Esther instinctively took it. She was expecting to see the last 24 hours of this Man's life, but it didn't work. Quizzically, she looked at their hands, clasped. His was solid, but hers was not. His skin had a radiance that was bright and clean, but fresher, and seemed to be full of energy and light. There were thick scars too. Surely this couldn't be the "Jesus" she had heard about… or could it?

Esther thought to herself, "Am I dead?" She looked into the eyes of the Man before her. They were like fire. Well, not exactly like fire, but that's the only way to describe them. They were brilliantly bright and seemed to have all of the colors of the rainbow in the iris part of His eyes. Esther had never seen eyes like this before. Light seemed to emanate from His eyes like beams of love.

His eyes also seemed to pierce into her very soul and fill her up with indescribable joy and love. She knew that He loved her deeply and knew her perfectly and personally. She looked up questioningly into His eyes, and He smiled as he motioned for her to walk with Him; back toward a dark cave that was nearby.

Curious, Esther looked around her and could seem to see her life pass before the two of them. It wasn't complete images, but more like portions and glimpses of various things that had happened in her life, complete with feelings, intents, and thoughts. There were moments when a scene crossed in front of them that Esther was ashamed of. Times when she had not been sensitive to her father's feelings, had unkind thoughts about someone, had behaved selfishly, or times when she had made a careless choice. These were painful to witness in front of this Being. Yet, when she hesitantly glanced in His direction, she only felt complete understanding and profound compassion, empathy, and love for her.

There were times when she remembered struggling, and she never realized that her mother, Ziven, had been there by her side whispering to her and encouraging her. She wondered where her mother was now. If Esther were dead, shouldn't she be greeted by her mother? This Being never spoke a word, but clearly communicated that when the time was right, she would indeed be with her mother again.

He drew her attention toward a specific area of the cave. She could sense faces of three children; a boy and two girls. She sensed everything about them as though she had known them for years. She knew their names, their personalities and character traits. She knew that she loved them very much. Esther was given to know that these were the children she had agreed to care for in this life.

As she pondered this thought, she realized that maybe she really wasn't dead. How could she have children if she were dead? Then she instantly understood that until she crossed the bridge she saw, she may choose to return to her life. Once she decided to cross that bridge, she would not be able to change her mind and go back.

The Being directed Esther's attention toward another area of the cave. It seemed to represent various things she had already accomplished, and many other things that she had not yet accomplished. It was communicated to her that this was her "mission" in life. She tried to decipher each of the elements of this "mission," but the image was taken away from her sight and she was given to know that she could choose to be led to accomplish all this and more. *"You have been chosen to accomplish a great work. If you choose to be led, you will know what to do,"* came a thought into her mind that pierced her heart. The solidity of that promise felt rock-hard and immovable.

That was her answer. She knew what to do. At the very moment that Esther decided she needed to return to her body, she took a deep breath and slowly opened her eyes.

Chapter XXIV

DECISIONS

It was starting to get dark. "How long have we been digging?" John asked Robert. It wasn't that he wanted to rest. Afterall, his mind and body had been trained to endure interrogation and torture; lack of food, water, or sleep for long periods of time; and other potential situations requiring extended physical and emotional stamina. Somehow this seemed different, though. He was just worried about Esther, and what condition they might find her in… IF they found her!

Robert stood up straight, his shirt drenched and filthy, as he wiped the dust off of his watch to check the time. "I think she's been down there since about 9:30 or 10:00 o'clock! It's 5:00 now…" His voice trailed off. He didn't want to think about Esther being trapped for over seven hours underneath a pile of debris from over a thousand feet of twisted metal and concrete falling down on her.

Then, a coughing fit overtook him. He hid the bloody mucus he was coughing up, and the pain in his ribs with each cough. "You need to rest for a minute," John said with genuine concern. "Would you?" Robert responded.

Robert and John looked at each other, forced themselves to take a deep breath, and began again the task of lifting and removing anything in their way. Robert's hands had become bloody from new wounds, but he didn't seem to notice. All he could think about was what they might find, yet he tried not to think about that most of all, so he began humming.

John nodded his head with understanding. One of the best tools to endure emotional trauma, and the self-induced torment that fear can cause, is to distract the mind. He knew the tune Robert was humming. It was a tune he had learned as a child; one of comfort and peace. He could sense his feelings about this man begin to change slightly. As he glanced over at Robert, he could tell that the man was frantic to find Esther… perhaps just as frantic as he was. *"Maybe he's in love with her too!"*

"Great!" he muttered under his breath through clenched teeth.

It was then that their digging had brought them to a layer John knew would be there, but didn't really want to think about. A layer he wasn't sure Robert could handle. John decided to help Robert prepare for the worst, but hope for the best.

"Hey, Robert?" he began. "Yea?" Robert didn't stop digging, didn't even look up. "I just wanted to prepare you for what we will start to find; for what we might find…"

"Yea?"

"Well," John chose his words carefully and tried not to be indelicate. "There were a lot of people in this building. Most of them will not have made it."

Robert shot John a fierce glare as though he was suggesting that Esther wouldn't make it. "I'm not talking about Esther, of course," John quickly added. Robert continued using his hands as shovels.

John continued slowly and carefully. "In my military experience, it is very likely that we will come across damaged parts of…"

Robert had stopped moving. He had stopped breathing. Then, he began trembling. With eyes wide with horror, he stood up straight with his hand held out. In his right palm was part of a woman's hand. In one motion he gasped, closed his eyes tight and threw the burned flesh to the ground.

John took a few steps in Robert's direction and reached out his hand to Robert's shoulder to try to comfort him. "It wasn't her," he weakly said as he tried to comfort the man.

Robert sat down on a jagged piece of concrete, put his head in his quivering bloody hands, and began shaking his head as he repeated, "No! No! No! No!"

Before Robert could start spiraling down the emotional path that would be too hysterically far to return from, John grabbed him by the shoulders and shook him a bit to get his attention. Then, suddenly remembering that his left arm had been in a sling, John shifted his grip to be more delicate.

"We can't give up! If she's gone, we can't do anything to help her!" Robert closed his eyes, and John shook him gently again to make him look at him. Then, he slowed down to give his next words more emphasis. "But if she's alive, neither of us could live with ourselves if we ever gave up on her! Right?!" Robert nodded.

"We're going to find things we don't want to see, things we don't want to think about. We cannot let ourselves give up! Do you hear me?! We can't ever give up on Esther!!"

Meanwhile, another 10 feet below, in a ventilation shaft, Esther regained consciousness. She was so tired! It was difficult for her to stay awake, and her head felt as though it had exploded inside of her skull and that her eye balls were burning! It would be so easy to just go to sleep forever. Just the effort to take each breath, seemed like more energy than she had altogether.

A soft-spoken thought came into her mind. It wasn't a voice she particularly recognized, but yet it seemed familiar to her at the same time. *"Esther. You have a decision to make. You may do nothing, and die. That is one of your choices. The other choice you have is to make some noise so someone can find you. You need to be found soon, or your choice will be spent."*

Esther's mind was foggy. She began to drift away again. *"Esther!"* The voice was no longer gentle. *"You must make noise to be found! There are people looking for you! Make some noise so they know where to look!"*

She startled at this and heard her bangled bracelets hit the metal of the ventilation shaft she had fallen into during the collapse. *"That's it!"* she thought. *"It won't take much energy, and I can keep this up as long as I need to so they can find me."*

With that, Esther began banging her arm against the metal. The collapsed metal walls created an echo chamber, and Esther realized that she finally had hope.

"Stop!" John shouted. Robert stopped digging. "Listen. Do you hear that?" he whispered. The eyes of both Robert and John grew with hopeful surprise. "I know it's her!" Robert exclaimed. "I sure hope so," John whispered. Then, the two resumed the exhausting mountainous task before them with more fervor than ever before.

Chapter XXV

MERCY HOSPITAL

The sounds of a hospital room are unmistakable, with the machines beeping, nurses chatting in the nearby station in the hall, and the occasional whirring of a blood-pressure cuff filling with air, then releasing and holding as it takes a measured reading. Yes, the sounds are familiar to anyone who has ever been in a hospital room, an emergency room, or an Intensive Care Unit.

Esther heard someone breathing heavily as though they were asleep. She slowly opened her eyes, but couldn't see anything. *"It sure is dark in here!"* she thought to herself. *"I wonder what time it is."*

She scanned the room around her, but couldn't even see the dim glowing lights that should be accompanying all of the machines she imagined were connected to her body. "That's strange," she whispered aloud.

At that, she felt a hand touch her arm. That startled her, and as she jumped, there were so many different areas of her body that felt a sharp jolt of pain; so many that she couldn't count them. She heard a voice gently say, "Esther."

This was different from the experiences when the Man in white had spoken her name. It didn't have the same layered effect of exposing every aspect of her life in one word, but it did have a profound element of love.

"Esther, you're going to be alright. Everything is going to be alright!" the voice said.

"Robert? Is that you?" she strained to clear the fogginess of her brain.

"You are going to be alright," the voice said as it trailed off.

Esther felt the last 24 hours of the man touching her arm. She saw Robert following the prompting to start digging for her, even though he had broken ribs and was still recovering from the injuries of his torture. She watched him hysterically convince the man with the excavator to join him. She saw Robert and John both digging desperately through the mountain of rubble, hands bloodied, and frantic to find her. She felt his worry and panic. She felt his love for her.

Esther blinked her eyes and shook her head slightly, but that caused a shooting pain down her back. "What happened?" she weakly managed. Then she felt a hand touch her other arm. Jolting at not having sensed another person in the room, she winced with pain.

"There has been a terrorist attack. The twin towers are gone," he said in disbelief.

Distracted by the sensation of experiencing the last 24 hours of John's life, she watched in her mind as she saw him protecting the President, then running to find her. She witnessed his frantic searching with Robert, comforting him as they dug, and something else. Jealousy was being put aside. John loved her too!

This realization was disorienting. "John?" she weakly managed. "What did you say?"

Simultaneously, Robert and John began telling her about America being attacked. It seemed as though one would numbly tell one aspect of what happened until he began to become overwhelmed with emotion. Then the other one would numbly pick up where the first had left off; and back and forth several times.

Eventually, detachment was replaced by fury and frustration. Both of these men were obviously passionate patriots. They did not speak openly about what they thought was really behind the attacks. Neither did they speak openly about their feelings for Esther. Not in this setting.

Suddenly, Esther heard someone else come in, and the question of why she couldn't see had to be addressed.

"Who's there?" she blurted.

A calm and somewhat cheerful female voice (with far too much animation for Esther's tastes) said, "Hello, Esther. My name is Doctor Tristy Henderson. How are we feeling today?"

As Doctor Henderson took Esther's wrist to feel for a pulse, Esther could sense the last 24 hours of this healthcare provider flashed in front of her consciousness. The overtly cheerfulness was not an act. This woman had sacrificed so much to become a doctor. Her family had disowned her after her husband and children were all killed in a car accident while she was driving. She had been drinking. After that, she devoted her life to helping others, and to do it cheerfully. She remembered this motivation to her purpose every morning in a daily devotional mantra.

"How are we feeling today?" she repeated gently. Esther didn't see the doctor shining a bright light into her eyes. "Let me know if you can see anything." she asked.

"Why can't I see? Am I..." her voice trailed off, unable to force herself to face the potential that she could actually be blind.

Doctor Henderson looked closely into Esther's eyes with a magnifying lens, then raised herself up and took a deep breath. She patted Esther's hand and then cradled it in both of her hands. "I need to do some more examinations. I don't want to give you false hope, but there's a possibility that your blindness could be temporary."

She let that sink in a little bit before continuing. "I'm ordering more tests, but I think it's a possibility that there has been some swelling in your brain that is creating pressure on the optic nerve. This is what could be causing the blindness. Once the swelling goes down, your sight should return." Doctor Henderson paused again as she continued examining Esther's wounds and bandages.

"There is another possibility I need you to be ready for," the young doctor began hesitantly. Brightening up, she continued, "It doesn't appear that there has been any damage to the eyes themselves. We'll do some testing to see if the blood vessels in your eyes are bleeding into the vitreous. Even if that's the case, that would also be temporary. The concern I have is that the jolt your body took when you fell down that shaft could have detached your retinas. That is the worst-case scenario."

The bright hospital room suddenly felt darkened and heavy with the weight of what had just been said, and all of its implications. It was as though someone had just snuffed out all the joy in the world, and all that was left was the faint wisp of smoke floating and twisting upward and out of existence.

Esther realized that she was holding her breath. This was one of those defining moments in a person's life when they can actually choose the type of character they will develop; choose the type of person to actually be. She remembered something her mother had written in her journal. *"'Becoming' is the process of 'coming' closer to who you want to 'be.'"*

Esther let out an exhale and closed her eyes, then quipped, "Oh! Is that all?!"

"Listen, I don't have to be able to see to tell that everyone is as serious as the tomb in here. If God wills it, I'm blind. I'll have to figure out how to deal with that. If it's temporary, then I'll rejoice when I can see again – but I'll have a better appreciation for those who really are blind."

The room was still silent, so Esther continued with a slight chuckle. "I'll be alright! I have a strong feeling that everything is going to be alright." As she said these words, she remembered the experience when she was buried under the rubble when she felt those words. She also felt that tingling and warm sensation sweep through her body that every molecule in her soul seemed to be quivering and reverberating that what she had just said was truth.

Tristy Henderson smiled and replied, "Of course it is!" Then, changing the subject began to check out the rest of Esther's injuries.

"Now, we've completed several x-rays, and all other injuries appear to be minor except for your left leg. When we did an x-ray on your left ankle, we found that the Tibia and Fibula are both broken. We're going to need to get you into surgery right away, before your bones try to heal themselves in the wrong positions. I've done this before, but we'll bring in an Orthopedic Surgeon I know who is an expert, if that's alright."

"Wow, really? I don't feel any pain!" Esther exclaimed. "I do remember feeling my leg and how soggy it seemed." Then, Esther wondered if her brain turned it off to save her from experiencing that pain.

After a slight pause, Dr. Henderson continued, "Basically, your foot is no longer connected to your leg, except with tissue. There will be several small plates in your fibula (the outside bone of the two) with small screws to hold them into place and basically re-create the support you'll need to walk. The larger of the two, the tibia also has a piece of bone that is broken off altogether. We can use two 4-inch screws to secure those pieces to each other."

Esther tried to lighten the mood with a slight joke, "So, will I get to set off the alarms at airports?"

"Probably not," the doctor laughed. "We use a titanium metal that is usually not enough to set off those alarms." Esther made a fake sad face at that.

Tristy paused to allow for any questions, then continued. "You'll need to keep your foot above your heart for the next four weeks. Then, slowly, we'll allow gentle pressure and discuss mobility as you heal. There will be several months of physical therapy and a bit of discomfort, but you should be just fine in no time!"

Then, in a more serious tone, she asked, "You will need someone at home to help you for at least 4 weeks." Looking around the room at the two young men who had brought Esther in, Tristy decided to leave it at that for now. She had other patients to see, more tests to order for Esther, as well as a surgery to schedule. So, with that she excused herself and left.

Breaking the awkward silence, Robert spoke up. "Can I get you anything? Would you like me to get your father on the phone?"

John scolded himself for not thinking of that first.

"He should be told something, but I'm afraid he'll come all the way out here to help me." Esther thought a moment and said towards Robert's direction, "Yes, thank you. That would be nice." Robert dialed the number and handed the receiver to Esther. "Do you two mind if I speak to him in private?" she asked.

"Of course not!" and with that they were both out in the hallway with the door closed behind them.

As they waited in the hallway, John began pacing. Robert took a long look at his rival and realized that this man loved Esther too. *"Fantastic!"* he said to himself. *"I get to compete against Brad Pitt!"*

Suddenly John spun around to face Robert and said abruptly, "Look, we both care about Esther. That's obvious. We both want what's best for her, right?"

"Right."

"Someone needs to be with her to help her 24/7. Right?"

"Right."

"What about taking shifts?" John started pacing again. Then, it seemed as though he were just talking aloud to himself. "If she doesn't want her father to come, we can help. There's nothing improper about that. She needs help, and we're her friends. It's just as simple as that. She would do it for us. It's probably what she wants to happen anyway. Then, if her father does come, we could just help take care of her until he gets here."

Then, stopping to look Robert squarely in the face, he said, "Right?"

Stunned, and still trying to take in the entire situation, all he could do was nod.

John noticed through the window that Esther had hung up the phone, so he bolted in with Robert following in his wake.

"I've got an idea," he blared. Then, noticing the sad look on Esther's face, he sat next to her and stroked her arm. "Is everything alright?"

"I had to leave a message," she replied. "I can't tell you how much it means to me that the both of you worked so hard to get me out," she said somberly. "How are your hands, and Robert, is your head alright?"

John and Robert looked at each other. Then John began, "How did you know…" but Robert interrupted. "You *saw* that?"

"Yes. When you both touched my arm."

Just then, a nurse noisily entered the room. "Just need to check your vitals and get you ready for that surgery. Can you tell me your name please?"

"Esther Cohen."

"Do you know what day this is?"

There was a pause.

"The date?"

"The day or the date; whichever you think you know."

Esther crunched her nose as she tried to think. As she did so, John smiled. It was that sweet expression he remembered liking when he first met Esther in Chicago.

"I'm not exactly sure because I don't know how long I've been out. I think the explosion happened on Thursday. How long have I been out?"

Robert and John looked at each other. Then, the nurse answered, ineffectually gesturing toward the men in the room, "These two brought you in on Friday. Today is Sunday."

"I've been out for three days?"

"Yes." Robert and John answered in unison.

Esther took it all in. A beeping noise broke the silence, and the nurse threw out a quick "I'll be right back!" as she attached the clipboard in her hands to the wall, grabbed some hand sanitizer, and ran out of the room and down the hall.

Robert sat down and scooted his chair closer to Esther. Then he gently took her hand. This surprised Esther, but not enough to get a response from her. It surprised John too, and he felt his jealousy begin to rise a little, as he took a long slow breath to try to calm himself down.

"We were worried about you," Robert said softly as he began to choke up. Then he cleared his throat, glanced quickly over at John, and added, "We both were."

Chapter XXVI

RECOVERY

As Robert and John waited in the recovery room for Esther to wake up from the anesthesia, the only sound in the room was of Esther's deep breathing, and the beeping of machines. Even with these sounds, the silence was deafening.

Robert had offered a special prayer over Esther before the surgery with John's assistance. As they had laid their hands upon her head, anointed her with holy anointing oil for healing, and pronounced a blessing on her, they felt a unity of purpose. Suddenly, the feeling of rivalry dissipated; at least for a while. The only thing either of them wanted was for Esther to be well and happy.

To break the silence, they both began at once, then Robert let John go first. "You know, we're all in quite a predicament here." He began. Robert nodded, not taking his eyes off of Esther.

"She's going to have to choose between us," he stated matter-of-factly even though it was tearing him up inside.

Robert looked at John with a start, sighed, and then looked back at the sleeping Esther before nodding again. "When should we tell her about her father?" Robert whispered. "I'll take care of that," John slowly said as he left the room.

The next few hours seemed like days for Robert as he watched Esther drift in and out of consciousness. It was slightly entertaining, though, because she said and did some funny things! Robert decided to start writing some of them down to tease her with later.

- Writing with her finger in the air. When asked what she was doing, she said she was "copying down the instructions."
- Pointing to the corners of the ceiling. "Don't you see the monkeys?"
- Giggling. "That tickles!"
- Licking her lips. "I like pudding, don't you?" When asked what flavor, she replied, "Chocolate, of course! Is there any other flavor in the world?"
- "Is this a water bed? It's wiggling!" followed by giggles.
- Moving her fingers together in the air, she said, "Where's my flute? I need my mother."

Robert enjoyed the stillness when he could just watch Esther peacefully sleep. He loved the way her nose delicately curved up. Her forehead was wrinkled slightly because she always seemed to be expressively using her eyebrows. Her lips were full and her lashes long. He took her hand and compared the coloring of her skin to his. Hers had brownish yellow undertones to it, while his was more of a pink color and a lot lighter.

He extended her hand to inspect her long fingers. He noticed the veins in her hand bulging underneath the skin. Then he looked at his own hands. The scrapes and gouges were beginning to heal, so he had removed the bandages. There were still a few places where he probably should have had stitches, but he had been more worried about Esther.

He was still worried about Esther, but this was combined with a peaceful feeling that everything would actually be alright. When she had shared her own feeling of comfort, Robert felt a familiar spiritual confirmation that what she had said was truth. He had learned to recognize that sensation, and to trust it with faith.

His pensive mood was broken a he noticed that Esther began to stir. Quickly jumping to his feet and rushing to her side, he began to stroke her hair with one hand, and take her hand with his other.

She softly moaned and blinked her eyes a few times, trying to focus her vision; but she would only see darkness. Her mouth was so very dry, and her throat was sore. As the fogginess of her mind began to slowly lift like a spring morning in San Francisco, she took a deep breath, smacked her lips a few times and turned her head toward where she sensed Robert was. Smiling slightly, she whispered, "Water."

He immediately gave her some ice chips the nurse had left and felt useful as he spooned them into Esther's mouth at her promptings. This felt good to him. Just the two of them. It was as if no one else in the world existed.

The spell of the moment was shattered as Esther softly asked, "Where's John?"

Robert exhaled languidly before answering, that he didn't know. Esther's disappointment was clear. Before Robert could fully digest that thought, John burst through the door with a wrapped bundle in his arms.

Esther smiled weakly as she sensed John had returned. As he touched her arm, she jerked with a start and a broad smile exclaiming, "You brought my flute!"

Robert caught John's eye and mouthed a question about Esther's dad. John shook his head as he handed the cloth package to the half-blood Cherokee he had fallen deeply in love with.

Esther's long fingers lovingly caressed the cloth and slid her hand inside the sleeve to feel the smooth wood of the sacred Bloodwood Flute. But before Esther could begin opening the bundle, she sensed that the nurse had quietly stepped into the room. Upon recognizing that she had been noticed, she spoke up and apologized for interrupting, stating that she just needed a moment to take Esther's vitals and prepare her to be discharged. John and Robert stepped out into the hall to coordinate efforts.

John began, "Michael is still out of it. I think we should wait until we get her home to tell her about him unless she asks earlier." "I agree," Robert replied, then added, "So, what about a schedule?"

"Well, I think we should keep tabs on how Michael is and give her regular updates. What is your work schedule like? Mine is extremely flexible," John began. *"Of course it is!"* Robert thought uncharitably to himself.

Nurse Edwards left Esther's room giggling and smiled at the two hopefuls as she left while shaking her head. "Be right back," she called behind herself as she rushed to the nurses' desk down the hallway.

Esther was sitting in a wheel chair grinning with her package in her arms bundled like a newborn child, her left leg straight forward bundled just as tight, but with her toes sticking out the top of the gauze-filled black boot. "I guess I'm ready," she sang cheerfully.

As the sunlight hit Esther's face, she lifted her chin toward the warmth and took a deep breath. The hustle and bustle of the center of the world had been shattered, but today, the air was clear. The world was still in shock, but Esther felt a sustaining peace that was difficult to explain. She knew she would be alright. Everything was going to be alright.

She also knew about her father. Although John and Robert hadn't told her yet, they had each touched her. There was nothing she could do, so she decided to wait for the proper moment.

While inviting the sunshine on her face to penetrate the molecules of her body, Esther repeated in her mind the mantra her mother had taught her was an ancient practice of the Cherokee people. This was not written in her journals, but she taught Esther just the same.

At sunrise, The People would gather daily on a sacred hill facing East. As the Sun would begin to peek over the horizon, a pulse of rattles, drums, or beaded gourds would commence. The more sun that was visible, the louder and quicker the pulsing beat would become. Voices humming would be added, louder and louder, until the moment when the full corona of the sun lifted from the horizon's touch. At that very moment, The People would shout, *"Hey!"*

Then, in a quiet moment of prayerful gratitude and devotion, The People would repeat in their minds the following, *"I promise, with all my heart, might, mind, and strength, to serve The Creator, all the days of my life!"*

This mental reflection brought her peace, but her mind was racing ahead to a moment when she would be alone and could play her flute. She so missed her mother and needed to talk with her. She had questions about SolMaize. She had questions about her father. She had questions about Robert and John. Yes, she just needed her mother!

Chapter XXVII

WOUNDS OF THE HEART

The days seemed to speed by with Robert and John taking turns helping Esther. Occasionally, they would all be there together, and to keep things from feeling awkward, Esther would ask about SolMaize and what was happening with The Cause.

Whenever she had a moment to herself, she would pull out her flute and play intently. Her discussions with her mother soothed her soul and helped calm her heart.

She never asked Robert or John about her father because each time one of them would touch her, she would get the sad news that there was no change. Her father had suffered a stroke and was lying in a coma in San Francisco Medical Hospital. John and Robert would take turns calling each day for an update and would let the other know, just in case Esther asked about her father.

One question still seemed to haunt Esther. This was a question that was very difficult to ask, and far more difficult to answer, but finally the elephant in the room had to be acknowledged, so she ventured.

"John," she began. "If I am to remain blind, how can I possibly help in The Cause?"

"Oh, don't talk like that!" he countered defensively.

"No, seriously," she interrupted. "I can't do what I've been doing. Once this stupid ankle heals, and I can get around, how can I be of any help?"

John took a deep breath and walked over to where Esther was laying on the sofa. He sat next to her and gently took her hand. Looking into her eyes, he said, "You have so many extraordinary gifts. Your value is greater than you realize. You mean too much to…" His voice drifted off as he cleared his throat. "You are too…" he stammered again. "You know how I feel about you, don't you?"

At that moment, Esther's eyes grew immediately wide. Her eyebrows raised high and with a surprised look on her face, she began to sob.

"Esther! I'm sorry to have upset you!" John apologized.

"No, no! It's not that!" she cried. "I saw… your aura! It pulsed, and I literally saw it!"

John grabbed her in a warm embrace and they laughed and wept together. That's when Robert walked in.

The news of Michael's passing had not come as a complete surprise, but the timing was certainly ill-planned. How could Robert tell this woman he loved that her father was gone? How could he comfort her when it seemed that she had made her choice, and it wasn't him? What would happen next? How was this all to end?

Using a mental bull-dozer to push all of these thoughts aside, Robert cleared his throat.

John froze, and Esther broke the silence. "You have news about my father, don't you?" she said somberly.

The next weeks, as Esther continued to heal, were spent primarily on the telephone with the Rabbi in San Francisco making arrangements for her father's Kosher burial at the cemetery near her mother.

She seemed detached and emotionless as she made all of the detailed arrangements and only had Robert or John write things down when her mind seemed too stretched and weary to remember anything.

When a package came in the mail with printed photographs of the funeral service, she laughed at the old-school methods of the aged Rabbi. Robert explained each of the photographs to her, then they sat quietly on the back porch listening to the cooing of pigeons and the sounds of the city going on with their lives as though nothing had happened.

"Robert," Esther began hesitantly. "Yea."

"I think I'm ready to learn how to take care of myself now." Robert looked over at Esther and saw that she was carefully crafting her next words, so he fought the impulse to respond and remained quiet.

"I can get around better now, and I'd like to be trained, like Hellen Keller did, to get around on my own and do things for myself."

"I understand."

"Robert?"

"Yea."

"I care for you deeply."

Robert gently took Esther's hand, and stroked the smooth skin slowly. "You know how I feel about you," he replied solemnly.

"I do. And I know that I can always count on you to be there for me. This gives me great comfort."

"But you've made your decision," he attempted to finish for her.

Sensing his resignation, Esther smiled and reached out to touch his face. Turning his head to face her, she tried to look where she thought his eyes would be, and whispered, "I have decided not to make a decision until I can take care of myself. When I can stand on my own two feet and don't feel like I'm a burden, then I can make other lasting decisions. Does that make sense?"

Robert simply nodded. Then, realizing that he needed to speak, he said, "You need to know that I profoundly love you. It's more than just an emotion. I…" he struggled to find the right words, even though he had rehearsed this scene in his mind hundreds of times since he first clapped eyes on this astonishing woman.

"You fill every particle of my soul! Any spaces in my being are completely occupied by your presence and the very thought of you suffering or sad almost destroys me. I love you more than what I've ever imagined was possible!"

Esther jerked in surprise. "I just saw your aura pulse!" she exclaimed. "How is this possible?" he asked as he grabbed her in an impetuous embrace. Not wanting to hope, he decided to simply enjoy the moment, letting it linger as long as possible, and just delight in the possibility that Esther might one day regain her sight; regain her sight and choose him.

Chapter XXVIII

THE DARKEST PARTS OF THE SOUL

Robert had just left Esther's side, reluctantly handing her over to John's care. Today, he had a meeting with Chloe Collins, HR Director in the FDA. Her name had come up as someone sympathetic to The Resistance. This is dangerous because having a person's name floating around can easily make that person a target for the other side to gather information with or potentially pressure into helping them as a double-agent. Everyone has something that can be used against them. He had to be extremely careful not to be discovered, and to be on guard for peripheral unwelcome activities.

Pretending to meet with Ms. Collins about an HR matter, Robert slipped her a folder with a small earpiece in it, thanked her, and walked away. Chloe covertly put the earpiece in her right ear, and activated it by twisting her finger clockwise.

"If you can hear me, cough twice," was the whisper in her ear. Chloe coughed twice.

"Good, so, I will walk you through some scenarios. Depending upon your responses, we may be able to help each other. Rub your nose if you understand."

Chloe did so, trying not to seem too anxious even though her heart was beating wildly in her chest. Surely everyone around her could hear it!

Robert and Thomas had the building under surveillance with their team. Just as Chloe Collins locked her desk and closed her office door, several suspicious individuals (including those known to be with SolMaize) entered the building.

"You've got to leave your purse in the ladies' room. We'll make sure it is returned to you." Chloe did so without hesitation. Keeping her iPhone in her hand and the keys that were hanging on a lanyard around her neck, she walked slowly toward the escalator.

"Get a drink at the water fountain. As you do, remove the lanyard from your neck. Then, sit down on the nearby bench." This was a very clear violation of company rules. She could be put on report for leaving her lanyard lying around. It not only had her confidential keys, but her magnetic photo/name badge to get her into high-security areas of the FDA. She could feel her heart pounding in her chest, and her she began to feel out of breath, as though she were running up a flight of stairs.

"Leave your iPhone and lanyard. You will find replacements in your pocket. We will safeguard your belongings. This is necessary because we believe you have been tapped." With security cameras all around, she had to be careful not to be seen leaving these items behind on purpose, so she found a company newsletter on the bench, pretended to thumb through it, then left it sitting on top of her phone and keys.

Her heart was exploding out of her chest at this point, but she was committed. She knew this was necessary to protect her children. Just as the new phone someone had carefully placed in her pocket while walking past her rang, she heard the voice in her ear say, "It's okay. You're clear. Keep walking out the front doors and answer the phone."

"How do I know I can trust you?" she asked urgently, but in hushed tones, while looking around and trying to calm her breathing and slow down her frantic heartbeat.

"Look straight ahead at the man in the blue tie and rain coat."

Chloe recognized him as the man who had handed her the folder with the earpiece in it earlier.

"I'm sorry for all of the "Cloak and Dagger," but I had to make sure you were not cross-wired and that you were fully on our side. SolMaize, as you know, has unlimited resources and may have been made aware of your interest in helping The Resistance."

At this, Chloe Collin's face went pail. "You could be watched by them, so please be careful not to speak too loudly, nor to make any facial expressions or gestures that could give away our discussion."

"Okay. What do you want me to do?" Chloe whispered, trying madly to get her fears under control.

"First, you need to sit down somewhere and focus on your toes or something down low. Try not to react to what I am about to tell you. That's very important. Do you understand?"

"Okay…" she answered cautiously.

"Your children are alright…" Robert began.

Chloe felt as though her heart sank through her to the ground. She began to feel dizzy and confused.

"Ms. Collins! Ms. Collins! Can you hear me?" Robert's voice began to sound frantic in her earpiece but then quickly changed to a calming, peaceful timbre. "Ms. Collins, your children are alright. You hear me? They are alright! Now, slowly take a deep breath. No visible reaction, remember?"

Robert continued. "We have reason to believe SolMaize has your children under surveillance. We have our own people on it as well, to protect your children. Are you alright?"

Chloe relaxed a bit and slowly nodded her head, feeling as though she were in a foggy dream.

"Good. So, we were hoping you would help us, but we understand if you don't feel comfortable doing so."

"It depends," she began, "on who exactly you are. I need to be convinced that I'm working for the right side of this thing."

"Esther Cohan was in the Twin Towers when they went down. We need you to visit her today before retrieving your purse and your other belongings."

Chloe's eyebrows raised and her eyes became large with surprise. "You okay?" the voice on the phone asked carefully.

She nodded.

"There's more. Please prepare yourself. Esther Cohen's ankle was shattered during the attack, and she's recovering in an apartment in New York temporarily until she can travel. Then, we'll bring her back to D.C.

Are you still okay?" Chloe began to feel overloaded, but nodded her head anyway.

"Her father just passed away in San Francisco, and there's one more thing." Robert paused. Not for affect, but because he had never actually said this out loud and wasn't sure how he felt about all of it in the first place. He was still searching for internal comfort.

"You care about her as a person, don't you?" Chloe nodded.

Robert blurted out, "For the time being, Esther is blind." He let those words sink in, then continued, "She may regain her sight, but for now, this is her condition and she needs our help."

As Robert spoke these words, he felt that familiar tingling witness that what he had just spoken was truth. This finally gave him the comfort he needed. Chloe also felt a warm tingling sensation flow through her body that truth had been spoken. This comforted her as well, and connected to the message that her children would likewise be alright.

"Anything you need," Chloe committed fervently.

John helped Esther into the rental car, then ran around to the driver's side. This, they had determined, was the safest and least painful way for them to transport Esther from Manhattan to Washington, D.C. She was finally able to put a slight amount of pressure on her foot, but it still ached whenever she lowered her foot for very long.

Esther remembered the time, about four weeks after the accident, when she had gotten out of bed in the morning to use the loo, and she actually began to sob! She was a grown woman crying like a baby! As the blood rushed into her foot, it hurt so much, and she was so tired of it hurting! It seemed that the cycle of pain and discomfort was never going to end! Sleepless nights added to the lower resistance to pain, and at that moment, in addition to the blindness and her father… it just seemed like the last straw!

Today was different, though. Yes, it ached, but it didn't hurt as badly as it had. There was definitely a marked improvement. It suddenly felt as if a healing switch were flipped on, and she felt confident that she would actually get better. She wouldn't feel like this forever! This lifted her spirits, and so did the idea of getting back to her own apartment. The darkest parts of her heart seemed to float away as they were heading toward a more familiar area for her to begin her Independent Visually-Challenged Training.

"Robert is meeting with Chloe Collins today," John began. "Oh, really?" Esther answered excited at the thought of bringing her mentor on board. When she interviewed with this woman, they just seemed to click, and there was an immediate strong connection between the two of them. She was a "kindred spirit" who Esther wanted to become close friends with from the start.

Esther relayed to John how she felt when she first met Chloe Collins; about her children, and the motivations she sensed in support of The Resistance.

"That explains a lot," John responded. "What?" Esther asked.

"Well, there have been some whisperings that she is being followed, and her children in Hermosillo, Mexico are being watched by SolMaize as well." Esther's heart sank.

"Don't worry, though. We're recruiting her and we've got our best men on protecting her, and her children too," John tried to comfort Esther. She reached her hand over to touch John's arm and said, "Yes, I know."

After a long period of silence, Esther asked John to keep her up-to-date on what had been going on with the investigation as she had been recovering, and while the world reeled after the terrorist attack on American soil.

Chapter XXIX

FROM HERMOSILLO, MEXICO

He woke them up early that morning and stuffed the little urchins into his Chevy pickup. Hermosillo was a large town, but neighbors watched out for each other, and he didn't want any neighbors to see them leave. It would be an hour and a half before reaching Guaymas. They would stop there to stretch their legs before driving the long 4 1/2 hours to Licuadora headquarters, just outside of Los Mochis, Mexico.

The sun was warm and friendly, not exactly hot yet. People of all shapes and sizes on the tourist beach at Guaymas were enjoying the pleasant weather. Families were sitting in groups pulling out tanning lotion and propping up large umbrellas. Others were settling in to read a well-anticipated novel. Women in bikinis lathered their bronzed bodies in preparation for another day of sun worshipping, while children giggled nearby as they built sand fortresses and moats.

Food vendors walked the length of the beach selling delicious octopus burritos: grilled octopus, coconut rice, corn, tomatoes, and spicy jalapeño creamy salsa. Tourists tethered themselves to motorized speed boats that would race out away from the beach, lifting the thrill-seeking vacationers up over 180 meters into the air, floating to their delight into the silence found there under brightly-colored parasails.

Oblivious to all that was happening around them, Dale and Mae Collins enjoyed running back and forth on the beach, pretending that the surf was trying to get them. As the little bubbles appeared in the sand after the salty foam receded, Tío José quickly plunged a shovel into the fine sand and called to his nephew and niece to come see. "What do you see here, my little ones?"

Dale and Mae helped their uncle sift through the sand, then jumped up and down with squeals of delight as they uncovered several small, nearly invisible, sand crabs. "This is what makes those little holes when the water returns. You know they are there even though you cannot see them. When you see the signs that they are there, all you need to do is dig to find them."

The words haunted José because he had noticed signs that he and the children were being watched. There was that black car that always seemed to be parked a block away from their house. The windows were darkened, and there were always two people inside. Then, there were the hombres with sunglasses on that could always be found lurking nearby whenever they went anywhere. Today was no different. When Americans visit the beach with full-length coats, sunglasses, and hats; how do they think they will blend in? José just shook his head. "Americanos!" he said under his breath.

He hadn't told his sister-in-law yet, but when he had more information, he planned to make the call. Besides, he didn't feel very well. *"I'm probably just coming down with a cold,"* he told himself.

José rehearsed the past 24 hours in his mind. The strange phone call late at night. The instructions to arrive at the company's headquarters the next evening. Then, there was the sudden acquisition of that cold-medicine company.

José had reported to his supervisor that he had discovered something unusual as he had been conducting his usual research tests. Licuadora began its genetic engineering of vegetables like corn to help make it more financially solvent for production companies. The ears needed to be larger, consistent in size, and resistant to pesticides, disease, and insects. It was an easy thing to do. Just change a few molecules here, add a little strain of the DNA from the insects and from the pesticides, and from the most common diseases. It didn't change the texture, color, or taste of the corn.

In fact, it made it much better and more desirable. At least that was the messaging. It was certainly easier to sell, and that was the main objective of the shareholders.

When José discovered that the gnome strands he was seeing and adding to the hybrid strains of vegetables were actually from pesticides and various insects, he began collecting information and trying to decide who he could trust with this secret.

At that point, José began to do some of his own investigating. He had seen some unusual gene sequences sent to his super-computers for analysis. They looked human! *"What would Licuadora be doing with human DNA?"* he thought. *"This doesn't make sense!"*

Afterward, José began to notice many more strange things going on. Emails were marked "CONFIDENCIAL" but had large portions blackened out. The lists of people copied in the history of these emails were involved with various seemingly unrelated departments of the company including: Political Impact, Feminine Healthcare and Sterilization, United States Farm Bureau Liaise, Clinical Labs, Pesticide Enhancement, Laboratory Marketing, New Patient Outreach, Pharmaceutical Development, International Law, International Trade, World Health Organization Liaise, Branding and Messaging, Public Relations, Animal Husbandry, Cancer Research, Genetic Migration and Familial Relations, Genetic Mutations Management, and Disease Control.

In particular, José noticed changes in these departments' organizational charts happening every few days. New hires were being brought in daily, while others were "retiring" without any celebration or fanfare. They just seemed to "disappear." In the 30 years he had worked for Licuadora, he had never seen so much activity. He didn't know what to make of it all, but knew there was something going on, so he kept a file with all of these details.

When his sister-in-law, Chloe Collins, had asked him to take her children temporarily because they were somehow in danger in the United States of America, José didn't hesitate. He loved his brother, and when he had died suddenly, José felt a responsibility to his brother's widow and their children. Besides, he lived alone, and the thought of entertaining two young ones for a while was appealing.

Lately it seemed that things at work were getting more difficult to manage though, and having two little children to care for was becoming more problematic. Especially since now, it seemed that there were always a few suspicious Gringos watching them. José didn't know if they were watching *him*, or the children. Either scenario was feeling more uncomfortable all the time.

As José pulled into the parking lot of a motel in Los Mochis, he instructed the children to stay in the room, watch television, and eat anything in the room, but to not answer the door, nor the phone. He tried not to scare them, but made sure they knew they would be severely punished if they disobeyed.

"I need to go to work for a few hours, and I'll be back with food. On my brother's grave, if I return and you have disobeyed, you will have to find your own way home and you will get no food from me!" Then, José smiled at the children and winked so they would know that he loved them, but that he was serious about expecting them to behave.

After making sure they understood that he was serious, he kissed them both on the head and left. Licuadora was not far, and he expected to be back within an hour. He just wished he could get rid of his growing headache and cough.

Chapter XXX

THE FINAL STRAW

As Esther was waiting for John to return with groceries, she settled into her comfortable sofa and reached for her mother's Bloodwood Flute. It had been so long! She had almost forgotten how healing playing that flute was for her.

As her fingers lovingly unwrapped the leather pouch, and her hands made contact with the smooth cool wood of her old friend, she took a slow, deep breath. She closed her eyes, though it didn't matter. Everything was dark now anyway.

Esther began blowing air into the flute and let it play the melody that it wanted to. As she did, her heart was filled with peace and calm because, as usual, the flute began singing praise to The Creator.

"I sing praise that I can sing again! I sing praise that I am alive! The daughter of Ziven plays me, and I feel joy! I sing this song of grateful praise!"

In that very moment, it was as though the darkness was lifted from her eyes. Esther could see a beautiful, lush, green meadow with wildflowers splashing their dazzling colors throughout the scene. Bright red Coral

Bells, brilliant blue Bachelor Buttons, lovely purple from wild Lavender and Alfalfa plants were blended beautifully with the crisp yellowish orange of Coreopsis.

Esther could feel the radiant sunshine and see the brightness all around her! What ecstasy! Even if this were to be the only way she could "see" again, it would be a welcome escape from the real world she now faced. What a beautiful gift!

"Esther. Esther!" Ziven's voice called to her daughter. "Mother!" she replied.

"Esther, I cannot tell you about everything that is going on because I do not want to risk the unique opportunity you have to grow in this very special way." Sensing her daughter's dismay, the spirit added, "But I can tell you that 'everything is going to be alright!' Trust yourself, and peace will accompany you. Surround yourself with people who care about you, and you will have all of the comfort and protection you will need."

As she heard these words, Esther immediately thought of Robert, John, and Chloe. To these thoughts, Ziven added, "That's right!" which sent that familiar warm tingling sensation that Esther was beginning to recognize as a spiritual confirmation of "truth."

Then, Ziven said something that surprised her daughter. "You will find that your gifts are not tied to your sight. In fact, they are quite the opposite!"

At that, the vision was ended, and Esther found herself alone in the darkness of her sightless world again.

John returned to find Esther holding the Bloodwood Flute to her chest with the mouthpiece resting on her cheek, and a peaceful smile on her face, and so lost in thought that she didn't notice him entering the apartment.

"You look happy," he said as he began to unload the groceries into the refrigerator.

"I am," she replied. Then, reaching out to take his hand, she drew him to her and softly said, "Come here."

Taking his face into her hands, she sketched the outlines of his brows, his square jawline with the slight dimple at the chin. She felt his lips, his nose, and his eyes. Then, she pulled him near her and kissed him tenderly.

Smiling, she said, "Thank you for loving me."

The moment was abruptly interrupted by a loud knocking. Then, the door opened as Robert entered the room. "I hope I'm not interrupting anything," he said cheerfully, but with a suspicious glance over at John as he stood up while turning away and touching his lips. Pretending not to notice, he continued, "Guess who I found!"

"Ms. Collins?" Esther stated in surprise as Chloe stepped from behind the door. "But how did you…" Robert's question trailed off.

"Some things are not tied to sight, Robert!" Esther quipped.

"Chloe. Please." Chloe stated as she closed the door and quickly took a chair near Esther. "My dear, how are you feeling?" she asked. "Please tell me about what you've been going through!"

Esther didn't tell Chloe about her special gifts. That would come later. Nor did she tell her that she could see her aura, even though everything else was dark. *"I guess that's one of my gifts that is not tied to my sight,"* Esther thought to herself. In fact, that is how she recognized Ms. Collins when she entered the room.

They spent the rest of the evening laughing and then soberly reviewing what had happened with the attack in New York, and how this will change their world forever.

Just as John and Robert were about to leave, Chloe got a phone call. It was from Mexico. Her face went pail as she excused herself to take it in the other room.

"That looks serious," Robert commented.

Chloe returned, and without saying a word, touched Esther's arm to say goodbye. Immediately, Esther knew what was going on, and asked her to stay a moment, stating that there was something she needed to talk to her about.

"Do you want us to stay, or should we leave?" Robert asked understandingly. "Chloe, it's up to you. I'm comfortable having them hear what I wanted to say."

"It doesn't matter to me," she answered, a bit distracted.

"There's something I need to tell you," Esther began. "You may not believe me, so I'll just have to prove it to you. I hope you won't mind what might feel like an intrusion to your privacy." Chloe held her breath, then said, "It's okay."

Esther began, "I know about José." Chloe jolted. "I know that the phone call you just received was from your brother-in-law, and that he is very ill in Mexico. I know that you are worried about your children, and that you are trying to figure out what to do, and how to get them while keeping them safe."

"How could you possibly…" Chloe began, bewildered.

"One of my special gifts is that when I touch someone, I can see images and flashes about the last 24 hours of their life."

Silence.

Esther continued, "This gift can be useful to The Resistance, but I have to be careful about who knows, or I could be forced to use this gift for the other side."

That made Chloe think of how her children could be used against her for the same purpose. She felt the bond between her and this woman grow as they discussed the options available to her for several hours that night.

José was in a hospital in Mexico City under strict quarantine. He had been told that he had some new strain of virus for which there was no cure yet. He said that he had been suffering with cold-like symptoms, but suddenly could not breath, had a high fever, and a cough. He said the children were being kept there for observation, and that he wasn't sure where they were because he didn't trust the people who were telling him these things.

José said that there have been some suspicious things happening at Licuadora Genetics, and that he had been collecting information. He also mentioned that he had been watched by Americanos for some time now, and was worried for the safety of Chloe's children.

He said some things that didn't quite make sense, but as Chloe repeated them to Esther, John stood up abruptly and began pacing.

"Are you sure that is what he said?" he asked without missing a step.

Looking over at Robert, John said, "Do you really think they would do that?"

"Sure sounds like it, doesn't it?"

"I just can't believe it!" John exclaimed.

"Can somebody please tell me what's going on?!" Chloe cried.

John sat down on the sofa next to Esther. "It's the SolMaize Prime Agenda," he said solemnly.

"The what?" Chloe exasperatedly asked.

Robert explained, "We weren't sure about it until now, but there were some hints and rumblings about a back-up plan to control the world economy and win the hearts of the common people by frightening them enough that they would beg for control over their lives."

"It's brilliant, when you think about it," John interjected. "Back in 1848, Karl Marx came up with the 'Ten Planks of the Communist Manifesto.' So many of them have already been implemented in the United States by others, that hijacking the rest of the plan for SolMaize's purposes is actually pretty easy to do!"

Still stunned, Chloe asked, "What are the Ten Planks of the Communist Manifesto?"

John began, "Although Marx advocated the use of any means, especially including violent revolution, he suggested these ten political goals that could bring about a socialist dictatorship.

"The first is to get rid of private ownership of land. In 1868 the courts interpreted the 14th Amendment of the Constitution to give the government power over zoning regulations, taxes, and other ways to legally seize land from people."

Making a large check mark in the air, Robert said, "That's one!"

"The second goal was to create a heavily progressive income tax on the people. The 16th Amendment of the Constitution in 1913, in connection with state income taxes continue to drain the lifeblood out of the American economy and greatly reduces the accumulation of desperately needed capital for future growth."

"That's two!" Robert said making another checkmark gesture in the air.

"The third political goal was to get rid of all rights of inheritance. The Death Tax is just another step in this corrupt plan!"

"Three!" Robert said, swinging his arm around again.

"Now, the fourth step can be interpreted in several ways."

"That's right," Robert interjected. "Confiscation of the property of all emigrants and rebels depends upon how you define 'rebels'!"

"Ha! Like when we gave the government the power to seize property after heavy taxes are not met in 1986, and then when the 1997 Crime/ Terrorist Bill Executive Order gave private land to the Department of Urban Development and allowed for the imprisonment of anyone labelled as a 'terrorist,' or anyone who speaks out or writes against the government..."

"Or the IRS confiscation of property without due process!" John added fuel to the growing fire of sarcasm and disgust.

Seeing the growing shock on Esther's and Chloe's faces, John continued. "Oh, they're going to love the next one! Right?"

Scoffing, Robert said, "Yea. This one's a doozy!"

"Number five is the creation of a national bank with exclusive monopoly of power. Do you realize that in 1913 when the Federal Reserve System was created by congress, we created a system that can politically manipulate interest rates, and effectively legally counterfeit currency?!" John was almost yelling now.

Robert continued, to help bring the volume down, even though this was nothing to take lightly. "Number six is the giving complete power of communication and transportation to the government. The Federal Communications Commission, the Department of Transportation, and the Interstate Commerce Commission…"

"And don't forget the Federal Aviation Administration as well as several Executive orders!" John interjected. "Right! And the USPS… The point is that where there isn't total control, there are federal regulations that essentially do control all of these areas."

"What's the seventh plank?" Esther asked hesitantly.

John continued, slightly less agitatedly. "Well, the seventh political goal is essentially the government control of agriculture. We have the Desert Entry Act, the Department of Agriculture, the Department of Commerce and Labor, the Department of the Interior, the Environmental Protection Agency, the Bureau of Land Management, the Bureau of Reclamation, the Bureau of Mines, the National Park Service, and the IRS control of business through corporate regulations..."

"You can't make this stuff up!" Robert exclaimed.

"I had no idea!" Chloe exclaimed, shaking her head.

Robert continued. "Well number eight is a kicker, and there are many who cheer for this one. It calls for the equal 'obligation' not the equal 'right' of all to work. Women used to have the choice to raise their own children, but the Social Security Administration and the Department of Labor have created the national debt and inflation that has caused the need for a two-income family. While the Civil Rights Act of 1964, the 19th amendment of the Constitution, the Federal Public Works Program, and Executive orders all have good intentions about helping women who choose a career, or who need to or want to work outside of the home, to get equal pay for equal work… I'm all in favor of that! Don't get me wrong! It's just that for some women… they would rather have the choice, and not be forced by societal or financial pressures. I'm just in favor of CHOICE, that's all."

Esther turned her face toward where John was. "And how do you feel about that?" she asked probingly.

"Well, part of number eight also says to establish industrial armies, especially for agriculture. What I see here is that the Equal Rights Amendment means that women should do all work that men do, including the military." He paused a moment, and carefully added more slowly, "If there were a draft, women would be subject to that, and not have a choice."

He paused again, not for effect, but to gather his emotions. "Some of the things I've seen, no one (man or woman) should ever have to witness."

Silence descended upon the room like a cold winter night and began to chill the group to the bones as they soaked in his words.

"I've watched friends incinerate before my very eyes; leaving nothing but their helmets and name tags behind," John said softly, as though he were slowly drifting off into a long-ago memory that he had tucked away deep into his psyche somewhere. "I was with one friend and saw him step on a land mine. We both heard the click and knew that there was nothing we could do to keep his leg from being blown off!"

Chloe gasped. Esther could sense John's trembling because with her heightened senses, she could actually feel the floor moving.

"There's just so much ugliness to war. Some women would be fine, but I fear that the delicate nature of some women would be damaged too much if they were forced to participate in and witness some of the atrocities there. I don't think anyone should be forced to live that, male or female! That's just my opinion. It needs to be done, but by volunteer means... not by force."

After an extended pause, Robert gently continued the list. "Number nine is to combine agriculture with manufacturing industries by gradually blending the boundaries of cities and towns and equally distributing the population. The Planning Reorganization Act of 1949, zoning, and Super Corporate Farms, as well as Executive orders and Public laws accomplished this. It's not a bad thing in and of itself, but when seen as part of this overarching plan, it is. And finally, number ten!"

Robert softened his voice to conclude this list of political goals enumerated by Karl Marx over a century ago. "Number ten is the establishment of a free education for all children in government-run schools, and the combining of education with industrial production, etc. If you have ever seen the political pressure on school boards and teachers to train youth to work for the communal debt system, the Department of Education, outcome-based education, the many unrelated tax laws that are intertwined with their own agendas..." Robert's voice trailed off as he became lost in thought.

The room remained silent for a minute or two as each person internalized the discussion and its implications with the SolMaize hunger for world-wide domination, and the protection of their secret agenda to make money at all costs.

Her mind still reeling, Esther asked thoughtfully, "So, what would the *exact* benefit be for SolMaize if the United States became a Communist or even a Socialist country? How does that fit into their lust for money and power?"

Chloe answered this one. "Well, when people are distracted by their own personal suffering – joblessness, economic turmoil, social discord, actually anything that causes uneasiness or unrest, even an attack like on 9/11 – they turn to whomever it is that says they can relieve their suffering. They look for a "savior", if you will."

Robert continued, "That's right. Imagine someone held hostage. It is their captor who brings them food. They begin to see their captor as someone who is there to help them; someone who relieves suffering."

"So, that's why so many victims of abuse end up defending or even loving their abusers," Esther surmised.

"Right," John added. "There's a mountain of data about that. So, now see an entire nation looking for deliverance from the very people who are causing their pain and suffering!"

Esther thought about that for a moment, then began slowly to put together the strategic pieces together. "If it were me, and I wanted to gain world dominance, wealth, and power… and it didn't matter how I accomplished this… and I already had virtually unlimited resources… and I was very patient and willing to go long… I would leverage any existing organization or situation to my advantage… I would fuel any fire that pulls the public to my plan… I would probably cause some major distraction if nature didn't give me one… something that would allow me to work behind-the-scenes to change whatever laws I needed to, or do whatever undermining would be necessary for me to advance my agenda.

"Like, maybe a world-wide pandemic, or some sort of fear of failing technology, or play on the fears that are central in the hearts of most people – like the collapse of the value of money. Well, probably all of these at the same time would most likely work the best."

Esther furrowed her brow and blinked her eyes, then raised her eyebrows high, and with wide excited eyes continued, "A pandemic would be brilliant because it could accomplish so many parts of the agenda at the same time!

"People would be quarantined to their homes to help stop the spread of the disease. Travel and tourism would be halted. Businesses like restaurants, sporting events, concerts, and even the personal-care businesses like salons, dentists, doctors, etc. would face closures because they could not maintain a reasonable distance from other people, and the public would be afraid to interact with them. Unemployment would rise. Depression, suicide, crime, and despair would ramp up for sure – just like during the Great Depression."

Speaking faster now, and barely breathing, Esther continued. "Politicians and terrorist groups would undoubtedly highjack the media and any protesting groups to ride the wave of anguish without realizing that they would also be helping to advance my agenda.

"Eventually, the people would cry out in one loud voice for rescue. They would practically beg me to control their lives, and would hand over all freedom of choice gladly in the hopes that I would relieve their suffering!"

Speaking slower now as the obvious correlations to reality and the actual possibility began to set in, she continued. "Sure! By creating a disease, and then offering the cure, I'd have manipulated the entire world and would make a nice profit to boot! I'd be the hero that saved the day, and no one would believe that I would have started it all in the first place!"

The four of them sat silently at that for what seemed like hours. Depression was beginning to set in. Finally, Esther took a slow deep breath and said, "Well, I'm feeling a little tired. I think I'd better get some rest."

No one spoke as they left her apartment that day. What else could be said? Even if it weren't true, it was certainly plausible.

Chapter XXXI

BLOODWOOD WARNING

She hadn't lied; Esther really was tired. She was emotionally exhausted. The conversation with John, Robert, and Chloe hit too close to reality. She could visualize each thing they discussed actually happening.

Shaking her head, as though that would keep her mind from thinking about such unpleasant things, she sighed and picked up her Bloodwood Flute.

Esther didn't need her sight to see the Native American flute her mother Ziven had made with her own hands. The barrel was long and smooth, except for the six holes that were strategically placed to fit the location her mother's fingers naturally fell along the ridge of the cylinder.

She slowly slid her long fingers lovingly to the end of the flute, and caressed the round opening in the end of the instrument. Her mother had to have spent a lot of time sanding every surface to reach such perfection. No seam could be felt anywhere. It seemed as though the flute was one continuous piece of wood, simply carved into the desired shape, not two pieces glued together.

The contours of the head of the flute were exquisite. Esther could feel the solidness of the wood as its perimeter expanded to make room for the whistle chamber. The "bird" rested snugly over the channel and the flue, because it was tied by a narrow strip of leather.

Esther slightly untied the knot, felt to check the location of the "bird," then tightened the leather strap to ensure the flute would whistle correctly. As Esther slipped her thumb to the tip of the flute head, feeling the blow-hole, she smiled. She was ready.

She took a deep breath and began gently blowing into the flute. It wanted to play a new tune this time. Esther could sense the molecules of the Bloodwood Flute rolling back and forth like an ocean wave as they fluidly bounced off of each other and created the haunting sounds of an ancient time.

Usually, when Esther played this flute, she would be visited by her mother's spirit, and they would converse; but today was different. Very different.

Esther opened her senses to focus on the molecules of the flute. She wanted to know what it was her dear friend was trying to tell her.

It felt similar to when she had stepped out of time during terrorist explosions. It seemed as though the molecules of her flute were slowing down so she could comprehend each and every nuance of their movements and their messages. It wasn't exactly the same, but it felt parallel to it. *"Yes, that's a good word to describe this. 'Parallel,'"* she thought to herself.

As the melancholy notes floated upward to the ceiling of her apartment, she seemed to be able to follow them through to another dimension. They led her upward and out through swirls and twists, through slides and shunts.

Suddenly, Esther found herself somewhere else. It wasn't exactly a place, yet it was. It wasn't exactly another time, yet it definitely seemed to be this as well. If it were another dimension, she would have to turn off her analytic mind so she could enjoy the experience and learn whatever it was she was supposed to learn from it.

Her mind strained to focus on where she was. She seemed to be in a place of light and energy, but few things were solid. She certainly wasn't. She felt warmth, and complete peace and contentment. The light she felt was brilliantly white, but her eyes did not feel strained. In fact, it did not seem unusual for her to be seeing with her eyes, even though she had been blind for over a month now.

The energy she felt was unlike anything she could ever remember feeling before, or had she? Esther felt uncertain on this point. Everything seemed more like a memory than a new event. Yes, that seemed to make more sense, or did it?

If she had experienced this place before, when was it? Where did this happen? If so, why could she not remember?

Abandoning questions she could not find answers for, Esther decided to focus on the message or meaning of it all. She relaxed and opened her mind to the melody in the background, and the feelings that had begun to well up inside of her. She recognized this as the melody she had heard in her mind last year when she had been driving cross country.

Suddenly, like a grand finale at a fireworks display, short—seemingly unrelated—flashes of ideas and thoughts pinged the sky of her mind from every direction, leaving as quickly as they appeared.

"This happened before the world was."

"Some rebelled against the Light."

"You fought valiantly in a great war."

"You made enemies in that war."

"You also made powerful friends."

"You were chosen."

"Along with others."

"You were courageous."

"You agreed to help."

"You are never alone."

"The Light will eventually overpower darkness."

"There is a divine plan."

"You are part of that plan."

"There are difficult times ahead."

"Things will get much worse."

"You must have faith in yourself."

"Be brave."

"Use your special gifts. That's why they were given to you."

"You have a key role."

"You will know what to do."

"You have been prepared for such a time as this."

"Everything will be alright."

The shock of that final message startled her out of the vision, and she abruptly stopped playing the flute. Her body was feeling that warm tingly sensation as she remembered being trapped under the crumbled steel and concrete of the World Trade Center. She knew that when she had felt those words at that time, it was her mother's words to her just before the terrorist attack when the world stood still.

"When the world stood still!" Esther gasped as she repeated the words of that thought out loud. Surely, that wasn't part of the SolMaize agenda. So many people died! That could not have been part of this secret society's plan for world domination. She shook her head again, but the puzzle piece did fit.

Chapter XXXII

THE SOLMAIZE PRIME AGENDA

The next morning, Esther was awakened with a start. It was Robert. He burst into her room and said, "I'm sorry, Esther! I'm so sorry to bust in like this!" He was pacing now and muttering something to himself.

Esther could sort of see his aura in the blackness of her blindness. This had happened before. Was this an indication that her eyesight was going to return? As she focused intently on Robert's shape moving back and forth, straining to see more, she had to shake her head to bring herself back to the present. He was saying something very important, and she knew she couldn't be personally distracted at a time like this.

That's when he grabbed her arms. Instantly, she could see images of the last 24 hours, but they were very confusing. Nothing made sense to her.

"There's been a new development!" he breathlessly exclaimed. Then, Robert seemed to be searching for the right words. He began pacing again like a caged tiger. "I don't exactly know how to say this!" A sudden look of fear and panic crossed his face.

Esther held out her arms and slid her hands down to hold his hands together, looking in the general direction of his eyes, she smiled weakly. "Just start at the beginning. Please, tell me what happened, and we'll figure this out together," she said.

"It's SolMaize," he began. "They've enacted their Prime Agenda!"

Robert began pacing again as he continued. "I can't believe it! It's really happening!"

"What?!" Esther asked tensely. "*What* is happening?"

Now, Robert was muttering to himself, shaking his head. "It's really happening, just like the simulation! Just like we were talking about last night! Oh, Esther!" Now he looked intently into her eyes, took a deep breath, and began explaining slowly.

"The SolMaize Prime Agenda is not only aimed at exterminating all the Cherokee people, it's Prime Agenda is much greater than that. It is a 'reset' of the world's economy, politics, and its population as a whole!"

Robert flipped on a local news station. Esther heard the broadcaster say that the borders between the United States and Mexico were closed. No one could get in or out. There was some sort of contagion that was loose.

"Chloe!" Esther gasped. "Right. Keep listening." Robert urged.

There had been a large explosion at a genetic engineering plant somewhere, and there was fear that some sort of virus escaped. A virus that had no cure. A virus that was extremely contagious, but only seemed to affect people with a certain DNA marker. The symptoms were similar to a cold. Some conspiracy theorists postulated that the entire event was no accident. Others argued that it was politically motivated. Still others shouted that it was simply the world cleansing itself of the over population of its creations.

"What is happening?" Esther exclaimed.

Robert urgently whispered, "Keep listening!"

"But…"

"Keep listening…" he gently interrupted. Robert began to stroke Esther's hair. Perhaps it was a nervous response. Perhaps he was trying to calm her. It certainly was calming. She liked it a lot. Then, her attention jolted back to the news report.

People of all ages and races seemed to be affected equally, so people were being urged to stay in their homes, not go to work, not leave for any reason. Schools were dismissed indefinitely, and curfews were placed in large cities across the nation.

"Oh, Robert!" Esther cried.

"There's more," he somberly whispered.

Face coverings were required for anyone leaving their homes. Anyone found outside without a face covering would be assumed to be a carrier, arrested, shot, and their bodies burned in a cleansing pit. This was called the "Zero Tolerance Antigen Containment Policy."

"Z-TAC" Robert muttered under his breath.

Travel between states was prohibited, and the stock market plummeted. Businesses had "Closed – indefinitely" signs on their doors.

"Well, that's it!" Robert exclaimed dejectedly. "It's the beginning of the end of life as we know it!" Then, Esther felt him plop down onto her bed next to her as he began to sob into his hands.

Now, it was her turn to comfort him. She reached out to touch his hunched over back, and combed her fingers through his thick wavy hair. He was struggling now to control his emotions, and at the same time, didn't want to do what kept coming to his heart.

Before she knew it, Robert turned to her and embraced her with his strong arms. He was shaking and she could feel his choppy breathing begin to slow down as he relaxed in her arms.

She felt comfortable in his embrace. This surprised her, but not more than when he suddenly raised his hands to entangle his fingers in her long unbrushed hair, and touched her forehead with his. He breathed in deeply, then kissed her gently, just near the edge of her mouth.

Swept up in the emotion of the morning, she smiled, and let him kiss her again. This time on the lips.

A loud knocking on the door would of course be John. Esther chuckled at the irony. Robert jumped up and went to answer the door, as Esther began to find her way to the restroom. It was going to be a long day.

After Esther had gathered herself together, she sensed there was someone else in the room with them. "Mayor Stevens?" she asked.

"Well, I'll be..." he stammered. "How did you know?" Then, interrupting any answer, he continued, "Well, that doesn't matter. What matters now, Miss Cohen, is helping Chloe Collins' children escape from Mexico before it is too late. They don't know it, but they have valuable information that will help us stop this madness once and for all!"

As Mayor Stevens spoke, his diminutive stature seemed to fill the room with determination. At the moment of his most fervent emotion, Esther could almost see a pulsation of light emanating from his direction. It must have shocked her a bit, for everyone in the room suddenly stopped talking and looked at her.

"Can you *see* me?" Mayor Stevens asked incredulously.

Stammering, Esther tried to explain. "It's difficult to describe, but I'm beginning to see auras of people, even though everything else is still as black as night."

Mayor Stevens sat back, and squinting his eyes, placed his hand on his short beard and began stroking it, deep in thought. "What other special gifts do you possess, my dear?" Almost at the same time, both Robert and John said, "It's okay. You can trust him."

Everything began to spill out. She told him about how she could see the last 24 hours of anyone she touched. She told him about how she stepped out of time and saved him from the explosion at the zoo. She told him about seeing different colors and types of auras, which seemed to help her discern the character of people. She told him about how she seemed to be traveling back in time to witness the expulsion of the Cherokee people. She told him about hearing voices of spirit loved ones, especially her mother whenever she played her Bloodwood Flute. She told him about the tingling feeling she sometimes gets when something she hears is truth. Having come this far, she also shared with them the impression she had that, like her name-sake in the Bible – Esther – she would be instrumental in saving her people; the Cherokee people in this case.

The room fell silent after she was finished. Mayor Stevens just sat there stroking his beard. Then, he got up suddenly, and said abruptly, "Well, in that case, young lady… I've got someone I want you to meet!" and with that, he stood up and strode toward the door.

Everyone, bewildered, stood up too. Robert took Esther's elbow to guide her as they followed the elderly gentleman out to the cars. Not wanting to seem disrespectful, John gently asked, "Sir. Should we take separate vehicles, and if so, might I ask where we are going?"

Like an absent-minded professor, the mayor stopped in his tracks and let out a gasp. "Why of course!" The group stopped too, and waited patiently for an explanation.

Shaking his head now, the middle-aged man ran his fingers through his reddish Grecian-Formula hair that had gone grey far too early, especially for someone in politics; but perhaps *because* of it. "Of course, you would need to know where we were going! How silly of me!"

John was to drive the Mayor and Esther, while Robert brought the other car and followed them to some government offices near Jefferson Memorial Park. The entire drive, Esther found herself chattering like a chipmunk. There was something about this man that made her feel totally at ease. It was the same feeling she would get when sitting on the beach, listening to the pulsing of the ocean waves.

He asked her questions about her mother, Ziven. He asked about her father, Michael. He asked her to describe some of her experiences when playing the Bloodwood Flute, and especially about when she stepped out of time during the bombing at the zoo—where she saved his life. All he said in response was, "Interesting."

"My dear," Mayor Stevens said as they got out of their cars and began walking toward the street. "You must never divulge the nature of your special gifts to anyone else. Do you understand?" Esther nodded.

Then, to Robert, he said, "Take her to the benches near the pond just north of the monument and wait for us there. You know, the area with the plumb blossoms, where they shoot lots of movies." "Yes, sir." Robert said with great respect. "You," Mayor Stevens said while pointing to John. "You come with me!"

Robert gently took Esther's elbow and led her along the circular walkway, around the pond, and toward the dome-shaped monument. Suddenly, the smells of vehicle exhaust, dust, and the busy city noises were replaced by the sounds of running water, birds, and the rustling sound of a breeze in the Aspen trees. Esther smiled as she realized the similarity these sounds had with rainfall or sizzling bacon.

She also noticed the clumsy and loud sound of her own steps. She had no idea that she shuffled so much, nor that it was such a horrid sound! Trusting that the path was paved, and that Robert wouldn't let her fall, she relaxed and just listened as they walked down the path.

Esther began to feel great peace as she identified various smells and sounds. Even without seeing them, she could hear the trees singing praise as they shimmered with the breeze. She could sense a butterfly, a ground squirrel, a couple of dragonflies, a hummingbird, the buzzing of some honey bees, and the soft laughter of a young family in the distance.

John reluctantly followed the mayor, but he was more than worried about leaving Esther alone with his competition. Scolding himself for his childishness, he focused on the mayor as they walked into the high-rise glass building. His attention was startled into focus when the mayor mentioned Ms. Collins.

"She needs someone to safely help her get her children from Hermosillo where they are being held. We'll meet you at the border so you can get across, but going in will be covert."

"I understand, sir."

Stopping and turning to face John, Mayor Stevens said seriously, "They are the key to this whole thing. This mission is top secret. Top secret! Do you understand."

"Yes, sir. Indeed, I do, sir!" was his absolute reply.

With that, Mayor Stevens knocked on a door that said "Secretary of Health and Human Services" and entered. The plush décor was indicative of status and privilege found among the President's Cabinet. Chandeliers, masterpieces of art, and lavish wealth surrounded the large mahogany desk where the Secretary's secretary guarded the door to the actual entrance of Dr. Albert Giroir's office.

The secretary was a nice-looking young woman in her 30's with clear porcelain skin and charcoal black, shoulder-length hair. Her smile was genuine as she stood to greet them. "May I help you?" she said with a lovely French accent.

Mayor Stevens, waving his hand so she would sit down said, "We're here to see the head honcho around here." At that, she looked around nervously, took a quick breath, then smiled again and said, "He's actually got a few minutes right now, if you'd like to go in, sir."

"Al-bear!" Mayor Stevens boomed as he burst through the elegant doorway. "How the devil are you?!" Then the door closed behind them. Robert had not been invited in, so he waited in the receiving area. Within two minutes, the two men came bustling through the door, laughing far too loudly, and smiling forced smiles.

"There's someone you simply MUST meet!" the mayor continued. "Oh, by the way, this is my nephew, Bob." Robert played along with a smile, a nod, and a handshake. Then he followed them to where they had left Esther and John.

"I can actually *smell* green!" she exclaimed with childlike delight. "It's wonderful here! Thank you for bringing me to this spot!"

"About earlier. I'm sor…" "Don't worry about it," she interrupted him. Then, smiling, she tilted her head as if to hear something specific. "That's the mayor returning with John, and someone else. Isn't it?"

"Why yes… but how?"

"I'm learning to detect individual footfalls, that's all."

"This woman never ceases to amaze me!" Robert thought to himself. He found himself gazing at her, and doing it safely because she could not see him doing so. He let his eyes follow the natural swoop of her auburn hair, the roundness of her high cheekbone, the gentle up-turned end of her nose, and the fullness of her lips… her lips. He remembered the tender kiss they had shared earlier that morning… or was it a lifetime ago? Then, he felt guilty and wondered if Esther would be able to sense him staring, and feel uncomfortable. Robert quickly looked away and smiled to himself.

He didn't notice that Esther was also smiling slightly to herself.

As the group approached them, Robert whispered to Esther, "You will need to make sure that you do not react to anything you might sense or witness. Any detection of your special gifts and senses could jeopardize the entire mission, your life, and perhaps even the lives of others as well. Do you understand?" Esther slowly and deliberately nodded as she took a deep relaxing breath.

"Well, this is the young lady I was telling you about!" came Mayor Steven's voice with introductory loudness as they approached the bench. Esther stood respectfully.

"Oh please, my dear!" came the voice with a thick French accent. "Please don't stand on my account!" his fake modesty dripped like sickeningly-sweet syrup. Esther sat back down, but raised her hand politely.

The plump French-man who was born to immigrants, took Esther's hand, and instead of shaking it as she expected, he turned her hand palm down and slopped a wet kiss on the top of her hand instead. The short bristles of his coarse moustache scratched her hand.

Esther fought the urge to wipe the back of her hand off on her pant leg, and politely forced a smile in his general direction while nodding a thank you to the man.

"It is such a pleasure to meet such a lovely young lady!" the man excreted. "De le plaisir est le mien, monsieur," Esther spoke in fluent French. Gasping in delight, the Cabinet-man started to sit down, but fortunately, Mayor Stevens stopped the man's descent and directed him back towards the direction they had come on an urgent matter.

Esther was visibly relieved, but also appeared to be quite troubled. "Are you alright?" Robert asked sincerely. Taking a deep breath, she answered. "I need to speak to the Mayor and John as soon as possible!" was all she could manage as she wiped off the back of her hand on the side of her leg and shuddered.

Chapter XXXIII

THE "PRIMARY THREAT"

Perhaps because of her blindness, Esther seemed to be able to focus on and remember more of the images she saw flicker before her mind when she touched the Secretary of Health and Human Services. Her photographic memory could collect even more information from the fragmented flashes. She could clearly see and remember something he had been reading earlier that morning. It was a "Confidential Master Plan."

As Robert guided her, telling her when there was a step, or when to wait, she let her mind review and make sense of what she had seen. It was a thick black notebook with dividing tabs. Dr. Giroir had pulled it out from a secret compartment to the left of his desk after using the combination 1776. There was a section called, "The Socialism Creed: A Plan for Control and Conversion to the New Mindset."

Sub-sections included 48 areas that had been carefully introduced into society over the past one hundred years. Many were the same as the "10 Planks of the Communist Manifesto" developed by Karl Marx that John and Robert had shared just last night!

There was a report in a section with the tab label, "DNA" that Dr. Giroir had spent a bit of time reviewing about the combined effects of Tuberculosis and Smallpox being introduced by Europeans to the Native Americans back in the 1700's. The report documents how these diseases ravaged the Native American population for centuries. In 2008, the incidence of Tuberculosis was still five times higher for Native Americans than for Caucasians. For those Native Americans that raised themselves out of poverty and increased their nutrition, avoiding diabetes, alcohol and tobacco use, their immune systems improved, and the instance of TB diminished. Additionally, she noticed, the instance of any type of cancer became almost non-existent among these individuals as well. The combination of exposure to these two diseases, and the special DNA markers in especially the Cherokee people, created what was called the "Primary Threat."

Just as suspected in the documentation she saw from The Resistance, an elaborate testing practice for finding people with the special DNA marker was underway. Unbeknownst to them, routine DNA testing has been done for anyone entering a hospital, anyone giving or getting blood, anyone undergoing any procedure or checkup where blood is drawn.

It was estimated that this process should cover the entire population of the United States within 20 years and the world within another 30. Special funding was being diverted from the alcohol industry to pay for this plan over the past 15 years. The database developed to manage this huge endeavor is massive, and great lengths have been taken so no one person knows all of the pieces of the operation.

Interestingly, the conspiracies to stir up distrust, low-quality education, and dependency on the government worked with many of the other tribes, but not the Cherokee. But the most disturbing piece of information she saw actually involved the cure!

"Mayor Stevens!" Esther began once they were all in the clear. "You're probably going to want to record the details I'm about to give you!" then she added, "and, you're going to want to sit down, sir."

Chapter XXXIV

LICUADORA NEAR LOS MOCHIS, MEXICO

John and Chloe found only an empty house in Hermosillo. It was unclear whether her brother-in-law José was just a terrible house keeper, or if his home had been ransacked, because it looked like a tornado had gone through the place. Papers were strewn all around, furniture was over turned, pictures were skewed, and there was some broken glass near the door.

Someone had gone through the mail and left a pile of torn papers on the table. A pillow in the bedroom had been cut open; its contents spilled out onto the bed. No, this definitely did not look good!

"Dale! Mae!" Chloe shouted! Quickly, John motioned for her to be silent as he pulled out his pistol and checked the house and its perimeter. "No one else is here," he finally said. Chloe, who hadn't realized she had been holding her breath, broke down and sobbed.

John put his arm around her shoulders and tried to comfort her, while still keeping an eye out for any danger. "Do you have any idea where your brother-in-law might have gone with the children?"

Struggling to regain a thread of rational thought, she wiped her eyes, sniffed, and took a halted breath. "José works at a genetics corporation called Licuadora, sort of near Guaymas," she managed. "We'd better get going, then. Whoever did this has a head start on us."

Something in the back of John's mind gave him a thought. He brushed it aside, but it kept coming back with the persistence of a summer hornet on a hamburger patty. *"Check your email."*

After making sure Chloe had something to eat, he pulled over to rest under a shade tree. Little urchins came from nowhere, asking if they could wash the windshield, shine his shoes, or sell him some "dulce de leche" candy. He bought some, thinking that if he ever found Dale and Mae, they might like something sweet. Plus, it helped him clear the children away when they saw that he had already purchased their wares.

He pulled out his phone and secured a connection through satellite signals to retrieve encoded email messages from secure sources. Sure enough, there was an email marked "Urgent" and "Confidential" in his inbox.

The message was from Mayor Stevens, but doubly encoded, so that even if it were intercepted, only he would be able to decipher the information. A date and time for something big had been set. "That's tomorrow at 1500 hours," he muttered under his breath after calculating the details.

"John?" came Chloe's voice with more than a hint of desperation and fear. "Do you think we'll ever find them… my children?"

Taking her arms and looking her straight in the eyes, John firmly said in a way that almost made himself believe these words, "Yes! We will find them and bring them home. By this time next week, you will be back to a normal routine, and all of this will seem like a distant memory." Nodding, Chloe took a deep breath and managed a faint smile, then got back into the silver Chevrolet Aveo they had rented for the trip. John got in the car, turned on the engine and the air conditioner, but did not take it out of park. He turned his body to face Chloe straightly. This made her feel a bit anxious, but she decided to turn and straighten her body towards John as well, and wait.

"I received word that your children are being held in the main hospital at Guaymas," he began. Chloe wanted to react, but sensed that there was more, and she wanted to hear it all!

Surprised at her composure, John continued, "They are both in isolation there." Chloe numbly forced herself to wait for the entire message before falling apart.

Proceeding more deliberately now, John continued. "It seems that José died from some sort of contagious illness that is unknown at this time, and they are not sure whether the children were exposed to the disease or not." John surveyed Chloe's face for any sign of understanding about what he had just said. She sat there like a statue for what seemed like hours.

Stiffening as she fought back the emotional surge in her body, her nostrils flaring as she finally took a deep breath, she managed a slight smile. "Then, let's go get them!" she suddenly said as she buckled up and faced forward. "I have an idea about how we can get them out!"

John found the motel in Los Mochis where José and the children had been staying. He paid for another night and had Chloe slip in without being seen. When he got to the room, he found Chloe sitting on the bed, holding a rag doll, rocking back and forth, sobbing silently. "Mae's?" he asked. Wiping tears from her cheek, she nodded expressionlessly.

"We'll find them! Do you hear me? Everything's going to be alright," he said as he patted her shoulder and started searching the room.

After about ten minutes, Chloe heard John struggling in the other room. "Do you need my help?" she asked.

As she walked into the dressing area near the bathroom, she saw John retrieving a thick manilla envelope from a panel in the ceiling. "This is something," he exclaimed! As they quickly reviewed it, she couldn't make heads nor tails out of it, but it seemed to make John very excited. He just kept repeating, "This is something! Now, this is something!"

On their way to the hospital, Chloe shared her idea about how to get the kids out. "I know this sounds cheesy, but we'll need to find some scrubs and snatch some ID badges, and..."

John closed his eyes and smiled, shaking his head. "Or, you could create a diversion, and I could sneak in and get them." She looked up, thinking for a moment, then smiled and nodded. "Yea, I guess that's a better plan. I must have watched too many movies, and it feels like we're in a movie right now! I just can't believe this is all really happening!" John gave Chloe a comforting shoulder hug. "Everything will be alright. I promise!" he said, hoping with everything inside of him that he was right.

Just as they approached the hospital, people seemed to be coming outside from every building. Each had the same expression on their faces: wide-eyes, open mouth, and disbelief. As John and Chloe turned to see what everyone was looking at, their expressions became the same as those around them.

Looming in the southern horizon was a huge mushroom-shaped cloud rising up a mile into the air. "This is it!" John shouted as he grabbed Chloe's arm and rushed her through the crowds into the hospital. "This is just the type of diversion we need!" he whispered excitedly as they ran, searching from room to room.

"Dale! Mae!" they both shouted as they ran through the maze of rooms and hallways. No healthcare workers could be seen anywhere. A middle-aged woman wearing a hospital gown appeared to have disconnected her trailing wires from a machine, and was running down the hallway toward the main exit. An elderly man, still connected to an IV machine was trying to exit in the same direction, but was knocked down by the running woman. Someone was calling out for help in another room just ahead.

"What is going on here?" Chloe asked John incredulously.

"I don't know! Let's just keep searching," was all he could manage.

The hallways were cluttered with beds and equipment pushed up against both sides of each wall, all except one hallway. John quickly took Chloe's arm and directed her to face the unusually wide entry with double red doors. Chloe's eyes got even wider as she stood there looking at the vacant entrance way. John whispered, which immediately got her attention, "I have a feeling they are behind those doors."

"You do?" she was pleading now.

"It's just a feeling. Do you remember what I said?"

Flustered and confused now, Chloe looked at John with furrowed and questioning brows. "Everything is going to be alright…Everything's going to be alright…" she repeated slowly, but obviously not convinced.

"That's right! Everything is going to be alright!" John repeated while piercing through the fog that had suddenly clouded her mind. "I need you to stay right here!" Chloe nodded absently and backed up to lean against the wall.

She watched as John stealthily and silently made his way to the red swinging doors. There was a small window in each of them. John peeked into one of them briefly, checked the perimeters of each door for any type of incendiary devices or trip wires, and was instantly gone.

He didn't know what he would find, and if the children were there, he didn't know what condition they would be in. He calculated that Chloe would be safer in the hallway than entering the Instalación de Prueba or "Testing Facility" area.

The documents he had found in José's apartment mentioned red doors and John had that feeling about the children. Resisting the temptation to find more evidence and information, he kept searching. *"Where are they?"* he silently shouted.

Immediately, his attention was pointed to what looked like a closet door with no signage. He felt drawn to it like being caught in the current of a fast-moving river.

As he attempted to open the door, it was obvious that it was locked. Looking around quickly, John used all of his pent-up rage at the entire situation and essentially ripped the gears of the door, and threw it open.

A dark stairway going down revealed a faint bluish light in the distance. Forgetting all of his training, John called out, "Dale! Mae! Are you down here?"

A muffled cry could just barely be heard. John leapt down the stairs, hoping above all hope that he would find them.

In the hallway above, Chloe had begun pacing as the time seemed to creep by slowly. She never was a fingernail biter, but this seemed like a good time. When she heard the demolishing of the door, and John crying out for her children, she could not contain herself. She found herself following John into the darkness of the basement.

"Stay there, and watch the door!" he barked. Instinctively, she obeyed, looking around frantically for any sign of discovery.

"They're here!" he called up. "They're okay, but they are weak. You'll need to come down here. Prop the door open."

Chloe found a black tote bag nearby and plopped it down in front of the door. As her eyes adjusted to the darkness below, she gasped as realized that what she was seeing was a large room full of hospital beds. Each bed was lumpy, obviously with a person underneath the sheets. Some seemed to be children, others were the size of adults. Each person was connected with wires and tubes to machines that appeared to be working on battery power only, for there were no other lights on in the darkness.

"What is all of this?" she whispered. "It's the secret José paid his life to reveal," John somberly answered.

"Mama?" a soft voice managed.

"Mae!" Chloe ran to her daughter in the blackness. As she did so, her foot caught on something solid; something soft; something dead. She fell as if in slow motion and never felt her head hit the floor. Perhaps it was because she was watching her life flash before her eyes.

She relived the day she met Principle Chief Powell and how they fell in love. She recalled the wedding ceremony, then later when she gave birth to Dale and to Mae. She remembered every detail of their life together, and how her beloved Noah had been mysteriously killed.

As the thought of his love filled her heart, she thought she could hear him calling to her. It seemed surreal, yet completely natural for her to hear his voice.

"Chloe, my child." She sensed herself turning toward the voice, and seemed to see the room growing brighter near His voice. "Come."

With that simple word, the residual feeling that "Everything will be alright" was echoed. She felt herself pulled toward the voice and the light… forgetting everything else. Chloe suddenly was wrapped up inside of joy, as though it were something tangible, and she was gone.

"Mama?" the small voice called out weakly.

John went to Chloe's side, felt her neck for a pulse, and slumped down as he whispered half to himself, "Everything is going to be alright. I promise!"

Chapter XXXV

UNIVERSAL STUDIOS – ORLANDO, FLORIDA

The air was crisp and clear with a few wispy clouds in the sky. Esther had her arm wrapped around Robert's arm for stability as she walked with a carefree presence along the cobble-stone walkway of Harry Potter World. Any observer would not know that she was blind because she made a good show of looking around, pointing, and laughing as though she were having a marvelous time.

Robert was carefully playing along, but scanning the faces of everyone they passed for any sign of recognition or danger. He had to put his own feelings aside, or he knew he would be putting the very woman he loved in danger.

John followed behind as well. He also had to put aside his personal feelings in order to protect Esther. He stayed close, but not close enough to hear their conversations, just close enough to sense any change in energy.

Esther smiled briefly to herself as she assessed this awkward situation. *"What am I going to do?!"* she thought to herself. *"I need a mother's advice."*

Then, re-focusing on the task at hand, she giggled as though Robert had said something funny.

She mentally processed how John had come to her hotel room and sobbed in her arms as he told her about Chloe, José, Dale, and Mae. He described in great detail the narrow escape he had made with the children as he hid them inside a blanket and literally drove them through the southern border of the United States without any questions or inspection. She remembered how John seemed to drift far away as he shared his promise to Chloe that "everything would be alright" and that he desperately wanted her children to have safe and happy lives going forward.

Later that day, she heard John telling Mayor Stevens about the evidence he had found in José's bathroom. This seemed to be all the documentation they needed to take out the main players in SolMaize, but John and Mayor Stevens were not convinced that they had enough evidence to actually put them away for good.

Roger stopped and turned Esther toward himself and softly said, "I know we are supposed to be play-acting here... but I want you to know how I really do feel about you." Being keenly aware of John's eyes on the conversation, and how he may be feeling, she quickly looked in John's general direction and said, "We'll talk about this later, Robert. I promise!"

This was a promise Esther definitely intended to keep, she just didn't know what she would say! There were so many things she liked about both Robert and John. Some things about them are similar, and other things are direct opposites. But, it's more than these things... it's how she feels when she is with each of them that is so confusing!

When she is with Robert, she feels at ease, she feels adored and beautiful, but then starts to wonder how John feels about them being together.

When she is with John, she feels protected and safe in addition to feeling cherished and desired. Thoughts about Robert are more like an afterthought about not wanting to hurt his feelings.

The instant that she began to sense that she might be leaning slightly more toward John is the last thing she remembered before everything changed.

A black tote bag, like the one John brought back from Mexico, brushed against Esther's arm. She couldn't keep from stopping and gasping. Robert instantaneously put his arm over her shoulder and led her to a nearby bench as she struggled to catch her breath.

John had to keep his distance, but stood nearby, pretending to read the tourist map in his hands. "What is it?" Robert intensely asked. "What did you sense?"

Whispering, Esther asked John, "The black tote you brought back from the hospital where you found the children had 4 glass tubes with acid in them, coils and wires, a mercury trigger with a timer on it, a cheap cell phone, duct tape, sulfur powder, scissors, and a vial of contagion... right?"

"Yes, but how did... I mean, I haven't had a chance to tell you about that part yet," John stammered.

"The man I just brushed against has a bag with the same contents. His wife is being held hostage unless he delivers it to the operator on the Harry Potter Quidditch ride in two minutes! He happens to be a retired military chemist who has played both sides in the intelligence world, but got caught. He knows it is a bomb that will flatten and contaminate the entire state of Florida with the contagion!"

"More than that," John added. "If it's got the same amount of nuclear material as the bag I found in Mexico, it will contaminate the entire northern hemisphere with radioactive fallout!"

"What can we do?" Robert whispered desperately. John told them to stay put as he sprinted to the virtual attraction in Harry Potter World.

"I feel so helpless!" Esther exclaimed exasperatedly. "Roger, I'll be fine here... see if John needs help!"

"You won't leave this spot... no matter what?!!" he cried.

"No matter what! Please! Go!" she shouted, no longer hiding her fear.

Robert grabbed her shoulders, planted a quick good-bye kiss on her lips, then ran off toward the popular ride.

Esther heightened her attention to the sounds around her. She could hear children dragging their feet as they begged to go into Olivander's Wand Shop. She overheard a couple ordering some Apple Beer, then heard them laugh because it was really orange soda with cream and had no apple in it at all. A young girl was spitting out one of Berny Bott's Every Flavor Jelly Beans because she said it really tasted like ear wax! Another young voice teased her about how she actually knew what ear wax tasted like.

What seemed like hours were only seconds but Esther knew what could be happening in those few moments. She knew she could be losing both of the men she loved.

As John reached the entrance to the ride, he tried not to cause a commotion as he moved ahead to the head of the line. A woman shouted out, "Hey! What are you doing?"

Instantly, the man with the bag turned around and met John's gaze. The attendant at the ride grabbed the tote bag and disappeared into a maze of hidden doors and access panels.

John bolted after him, but couldn't push through the crowd, so he pulled out his pistol and shot into the air. This easily cleared his path because everyone crouched down, and he simply leapt and hopped over everyone.

Robert saw everything that happened and followed John into the labyrinth of darkness. Esther prayed for them both to succeed, and to return to her safely. As she did so, something inside her whispered, *"Not both, but everything will be alright."*

"Oh, NO!" she exclaimed aloud! "No..." her voice trailed off as she realized what this meant.

Chapter XXXVI

THE SHOCK WAVE

Esther knew that she didn't need to have the heightened senses that make up for not having her sight to feel what happened next. The sound was deafening, but was followed by a surreal disorientation and loud ringing in her ears. She tried to stand, but her balance was all off, and she could only fall to her knees.

It sounded as though she could hear cries and screaming filtered through water and from somewhere far away. Her head was throbbing, as she crawled to find the bench she had been sitting on. Her hands felt things that were dusty, warm, and wet. Blood?

"John! Robert!" she screamed.

Instantly, Esther felt a quiet calmness and a growing light around her. *"Am I dead?"* she wondered curiously to herself.

As the light became brighter around her, Esther realized that it was her vision that seemed to be returning to her! She looked around to see people who were stopped in various positions of reaction to the explosion. Particles of concrete and debris were floating stationary in the air. Of course, she knew from previous experience that they were still moving… only at a very, very slow rate.

Perhaps this is why she could see. Light waves are slowed down to a speed she could perceive. This would certainly be something to think about some other time.

She looked up to see a huge mushroom-shaped cloud starting to form. *"Am I too late? John! Robert!"*

Making her way through the statues, she became more frantic as she didn't see either one of them. Then, she saw and recognized the man who had brushed up against her. He was locked in the motion of running away and looking backward towards a specific building. Esther quickly made her way toward the large pointed castle he had been looking at.

That's when she saw them; both of them.

Robert was covering his eyes and shielding a woman with a child. John was nearby in essentially the same situation. Both appeared to be aware of each other, and working in tandem, but busy trying to save the life of someone else.

Esther began moving all particles with trajectories to hit them as fast as possible. She noticed, however, that even with her increased speed, she was unable to keep up with the growing number of particles and the rate of their speed that was also snowballing.

Eventually, she knew she would need to move everyone out because the building would collapse.

A large structural I-beam started to move toward Roger, and a great chunk of concrete began to make its way toward John. Esther knew she could not move the course of these objects. They were too heavy. She also surmised that she didn't have the strength, nor the time, to move both of these men out of harm's way either.

In the flash that seemed to last an eternity, Esther attempted to push Robert over, with the intent to then save John.

She shoved and grunted, realizing that it would take far more time and energy than she had available. She looked around quickly to see if there were any resources that she could use to at least save his life, even if he got injured. There were none.

That's when she had to make the decision. It had come to this. She couldn't save both of them, so she had to choose, and she had to do it now!

She looked into Robert's face one last time, etching it into her memory forever, then rushed to John's side, worried that she may have wasted precious time and might not be able to save him either.

She found a piece of rebar on the ground and began hitting the approaching concrete, chipping some of it away. "This might just work!" she encouraged herself. She continued knocking off more and more pieces, until it was clear that it would no longer be a danger to John. She pulled the little child clear, just in case, and looked back over at Robert.

The large metal beam had just made contact, but it was clear that he had saved the mother and child.

That's when things began to get dark again.

Chapter XXXVII

DARK CLOUDS LIFTING

The next morning, Esther was awakened with a start. It was Robert. No, that was a dream; a dream about a memory.

She lay in a hospital bed in the darkness, but could hear the soft snoring of someone nearby. The beeping of monitoring devices could be heard. The smell of disinfectant was pungent.

"Oh, Robert!" she said aloud as she became fully awake.

Instantly, John was at her side. "You're alright! Everything is going to be alright."

As he touched her arm to comfort her, she knew. She knew everything.

John had seen Robert follow him and was angry that he had left Esther alone. At the same time, he was grateful for the help because he realized he was too late to stop the bomb from going off. He had managed to remove and protect the nuclear material, but the bomb was still going to go off. He realized, too late, that it would still have a similar affect, but not as deadly with radioactive fallout as intended. The contagion was deployed! He felt like a failure.

This particular bomb was a secret prototype design he had studied, but had never actually seen. Several countries had the interest and funding to create a bomb like this, but only two had the ability; the United States of America and Russia.

She also sensed his dismay at hearing her call out Robert's name. After the explosion, he had run to Robert, but could not save him. The woman and child he had been protecting were alive, but suffered a concussion and some scrapes and bruises.

John had watched the life flow out of Robert after he managed to say, "Take care of her!" Then he was gone.

That's when his own concussion began to make his head swirl, and his only thought was to find Esther. He turned to make his way back to where he had left her, only to find her lying unconscious on the floor near him, covered with dust and debris!

He scooped her up into his arms and sobbed with relief that she was alive, but quickly realized that she was not alright.

The next hour was spent rushing her to the hospital and pacing the floor while doctors performed various tests. He called Mayor Stevens, who was on his way, and eventually lost consciousness in the chair waiting for Esther to wake up.

She sensed his profound love for her and his devastation at thinking that she was lost. This compounded the pain of hearing her call out Robert's name as she awoke.

Attempting to heal the situation, she continued. "I couldn't save Robert! I tried to save you both, but I couldn't do it!"

John let that sink in a little bit. *"Wait,"* he thought. *"That means she had to choose… and she chose me! Don't be so selfish! She is hurting right now, and a man died today!"*

"I'm so sorry, Esther!" he tried to console her. "I can't imagine how you must be feeling right now. Why don't you tell me what happened?"

They both knew that she already knew his story because of her special gift when he touched her arm. So, it was especially sweet for them to both tell each other how they felt about one another, and to talk about what had happened.

Just then, Mayor Stevens entered the room. "I hope I'm not interrupting anything!" he said with a chuckle. John didn't drop Esther's hands, nor did she try to let go.

"We were just processing all that has happened," Esther smiled.

"Well, I'm glad to see you with a little bit of color in your face, young lady! You had us worried there for a minute," he boomed loudly.

"Sorry to worry you, sir!" she replied.

"No problem at all! I just wanted to let you know that you both did good today!"

"Sir?" John probed. "But, the contagion… It is out there!"

"I have it on good authority that it is not worse than the common flu. Nothing to worry about, my boy!"

"Well, that's a relief!" John looked into Esther's eyes and saw her looking directly into his.

"Esther! You can see me?"

"What?" Mayor Stevens added exuberantly.

She blinked her eyes a few times, looked around the room; looked over at Mayor Stevens and winked. Then, she sat up slowly, looked directly into John's eyes, pulled him closer and kissed him warmly on the lips.

Then, she smiled at the mayor and winked again. They both began laughing at the shocked look on John's face.

"Oh! Ouch! Don't make me laugh!" Esther exclaimed as she plopped back down on the pillows, holding her ribs.

Chapter XXXVIII

A NEW HOPE

Esther was finally back in her apartment. It had been so long since she had been there, that her plants had died, but that was the least of her worries. She had a lot of decisions to make; decisions about her future, about Chloe's children, about John, about her job… Lots of big decisions.

As she began cleaning up the dried, fallen leaves, and throwing away the light, dry soil… she noticed the Bloodwood Flute waiting for her patiently on the shelf.

Joy filled her soul as she slowly caressed the smoothness of her old friend. She could sense that it missed her too, so she sat down deliberately on the side of the bed and brought the mouthpiece of the Native American flute her mother had made to her lips.

She inhaled a long deep breath and began to blow, letting the flute play whatever melody it wanted to.

"I feel joy, so I sing praise to The Creator! I rejoice that I am still alive! I rejoice that the daughter of my Ziven plays me! I sing joyful praise! I sing honor, praise, glory, and joy to The Creator of all things!"

As Esther played, she connected with the Bloodwood Flute more completely than she ever had before. Each molecule and element within it spoke to her, reverberated within her soul, and seemed to carry her away to another place and time.

Instantly, she found herself on a lovely beach. The gentle breeze was sweet with the scent of Plumeria blossoms. The sky was brilliantly blue with fluffy cumulus clouds floating lazily northward. The temperature was comfortably tepid, as was the water lapping at her feet. It was the perfect picture of tranquility and peace.

Esther looked out at the long straight horizon. The roundness of the earth was stretched out so far that it appeared almost flat. The various colors of blue in the water seemed to hide the life-and-death struggles, the myriad of ecosystems thriving and struggling beneath its surface, and the shimmering balance of life in its care.

Esther looked down to see foam-etched bubbly waves washing over her feet, then threatening to steal the sand below her toes as it retreated temporarily. With each wave, her feet sunk down deeper into the diatoms, sand, and coral remnants of the white beach.

The throbbing crash of water seemed to send out pulsar-like waves with these words: *love, peace, joy, love, peace, joy…* Esther drew in a deep breath filled with contentment and delight, then noticed that she was not alone.

"Mother!" Esther seemed to run effortlessly to meet the slender figure approaching her. Then, she stopped cold. Another figure joined her mother. "Abba?" Esther cried in disbelief.

"What?" Michael laughed. "You didn't think they would let me see your mother in the next life?"

"Well..." Esther stammered. "I…"

"It's alright!" Ziven placed her hand on Esther's shoulder to relieve her from answering.

"You have some important decisions before you, don't you?"

Esther nodded. She told her parents about how she had tried to decide between Robert and John, and how she had been leaning toward John, but had to make a real, life-or-death decision… and had made her decision. Now that choice might actually mean marriage and choosing to be with John the rest of her life.

She told her parents that she didn't believe in trial or temporary coupling. She wanted to make sure that the decision she made was the best one, and that it was going to work out for the rest of her life.

Michael and Ziven continued to smile and nod as Esther poured her heart out to them.

She expressed how she felt about Robert, including the guilt that she didn't choose to save him in the end. She told them about how John let her know Robert's last words… to take care of her. Esther didn't know how she could ever fully recover from that horrible moment.

Then she told them about Dale and Mae, and how they had no parents. They were so such sweet and GOOD kids. They needed a caring home, and she already loved them so much. She struggled to get the words out, but finally admitted that the thought had crossed her mind to adopt them. She could teach them about their Cherokee heritage.

Michael and Ziven quietly let Esther get everything out first. If they didn't wait patiently, it was clear that Esther would not have been able to admit everything she was facing.

Chloe was more than her boss; she was her friend; and now she was gone. There was that sorrow… but also the uncertainty about her job, and the connection she had with Chloe's children.

"I know that I've been given these gifts for a reason, and that this purpose has to do with saving the Cherokee people. I think I've done this, and if I take on the task of raising Dale and Mae, I don't want it to be half-hearted. I will need to devote myself to their security and their happiness."

After a moment, Esther closed her eyes, nodded her head. There was that tingling sensation again, the one that means *truth*. She said, "It's funny. You don't have to say a word, and I know what I should do."

At that, Esther found herself back in her apartment, holding the Bloodwood Flute, and smiling. She knew it was smiling back at her, for it knew all of her secrets.

Chapter XXXIX

DECISIONS

John paced the floor like a caged tiger, back and forth, back and forth. It couldn't be that he was nervous, could it? After all, he had excelled in the Marine EOD training, psychological preparation for torture, parachuted in the dark, climbed under aircraft carriers to de-bomb them with only a foot of ocean water to maneuver in. He had faced the atrocities of war and watched people incinerate before his very eyes. He had seen the jeeps in front of him and just behind him fly up in incendiary flames, and held his friends as he watched the life drain from their eyes. Why was he… yes… *nervous*?!

He took a deep breath and tried to center himself. Instantly, he remembered the first time he saw Esther. He was getting a Chicago Dog, when the most captivating "Ginger" walked right into his heart. He knew he would never be the same, and he knew he could not live without her. Adrenaline began pumping as he rehearsed what he would say.

John looked at the mountain of crumpled papers that had missed the garbage can. *"I can do this!"* he said to himself. *"Just write how you feel."*

He sketched in his mind the color of her long deep copper-colored hair with that gorgeous blonde stripe near her left ear. Then, there were her eyes. Those stunning eyes that seemed to match her hair… all except for that fascinating golden pie wedge in her left eye.

Now, he knew what to say…

The knocking at her door would be John. Esther was nervous, but she didn't know why. Maybe she was simply excited. Yes. Excited was more accurate.

As she opened the door, John took a step back. This, by design, kept her from touching him and inadvertently discovering his plan.

"Nope," he said teasingly. "I can't surprise you if you touch me!" She laughed. "Would you like to come in for a moment?"

"Nope," he teased again in his best imitation of Rowan Atkins' "Mr. Bean" character's silly voice. "Less chance of you touching me and *ruining* the surprise!" Now they both laughed.

As they walked slowly down the sidewalk, John started to chuckle to himself.

"What?" Esther reached out to shove his arm, but his quick reflexes avoided contact as he began to giggle even more.

"What?!!" she quizzed.

"Just wait." John drew out the word wait as Esther feigned anger. "You'll see."

He led her to the center focal point of the National Mall. From this location, they could see the Thomas Jefferson Memorial, the Washington Monument, the Korean War Veterans Memorial, the Vietnam Veterans Memorial, the Martin Luther King, Jr. Memorial, the National World War II Memorial, the Lincoln Memorial, and the White House.

"Esther," John began somberly. Taking a quick deep breath, he continued. "You know how much I love this country… You know how much all of this," he waved his arms referring to all of the memorials surrounding them, "all of this means so much to me!"

Esther turned around slowly looking at each memorial and nodding her head. "Yes, I believe I do."

As Esther turned to face John, he was down on one knee. She gave him a coy grin and let him continue.

Trying to ignore the crowd that was beginning to form around them, he pushed forward as planned.

"I could live without all of this. For a time, I could even live without air, food, and water. But, I can't..."

"Oh no!" he thought to himself. *"I can't believe you are choking up! Get hold of yourself!"*

Clearing his throat, he continued. "I can't live without you being part of my life. If you say yes... I promise to protect you, to comfort you, to stand by you, and to support you. If you say yes... I promise to make you laugh every day, to say I'm sorry when I mess up, to never take you for granted, and to tell you I love you every day because I am hopelessly and completely in love with you! I know this sounds corny, but I can't help it. Esther Ziven Cohen..." He pulled out a beautifully wrapped gift box and extended it toward her. "will you make me the happiest man on earth?"

Esther pressed her lips together to hold back the ear-to-ear smile that wanted to escape. She carefully began to open the package.

"Oh!" was all she could manage. "It's beautiful!" Those looking on gasped as well. It was an ornate porcelain music box with an egg-shaped top that looked more like two gemstone feathers swooped up together to make an egg-shaped framework for the silver and gold dreamcatcher hanging in the center of the breath-taking swirling egg-shaped area. Dangling below the miniature dreamcatcher were emerald and diamond beads. In the center of the miniature dreamcatcher was a brilliant diamond.

Underneath the spinning egg-shaped dreamcatcher section was a gold and silver, inverted cup-shaped stand. It displayed a dramatic hand-painted Native American couple, back-to-back, with intertwined arms and upturned faces in a spectacular and unique way to honor ancient traditions and the spiritual power of dreams and of love.

Esther sank to her knees and looked John face-to-face; tears streaming down her face unabashedly, for there—in the center of the music box—was a hexagon-shaped black felt ring box with the Star of David embossed on the top.

Handing the gift box and the music box to John, Esther's trembling hands opened the ornate ring box to find a beautiful Black Hills Gold Anishinaabe-style wedding ring set with a delicate swooping feather design surrounding a large heart-cut sapphire surrounded by beautiful marquise-cut rubies and diamonds.

John set down the music box and the packaging and cupped Esther's hands in his. Removing the engagement portion of the ring set from the container, John set the box down. He looked into Esther's eyes while poising the ring to place it on her left hand, softly said, "Say yes!"

The pause was only three seconds long, but felt like an eternity for John.

"Yes!"

"Yes?"

"Yes!"

There, on patriotically sacred ground, the crowd around them cheered as Esther let John place the engagement ring on her left hand, and kissed him to seal the deal.

Chapter XL

GOING FORWARD

John couldn't sleep. Somehow, he needed to talk with Esther about the phone call he had received the evening before. It was another assignment. He had no idea how long it would take, or what would be involved. The SolMaize Prime Directive actually had been activated! The contagion in Mexico is not contained as reported. He had no idea how Esther would take this news, now that they had two children.

Adopting Dale and Mae had been such a healing thing for all of them. John just wasn't sure how their new dynamic would fit into this new world situation. Perhaps if he made a nice breakfast first; Esther hasn't been feeling well lately. He could break into the discussion with her after that.

Esther woke up earlier than she had planned. It was nice to lie there in bed, stretch, and dozily drift in and out of sleep until she was ready to get up. She smiled as she heard voices giggling downstairs.

She reached over to the pillow next to her. John was already up. That's okay. She didn't feel that great anyway. *"Ugh! I feel so queasy again!"* She quickly sat up and looked over at the Bloodwood Flute. She didn't even need to play it or touch it to communicate with it any more.

"Really?" she said out loud. "Oh…" Then she laid back down, holding her stomach, and sighing deeply.

She thought about the day John proposed to her, and the excitement of their new life together. She thought about how they decided to have a short engagement and to adopt Dale and Mae. The wedding was small, and a beautiful blend of Native American, Jewish, and Christian ceremony which made it even more special.

Esther agreed to continue working part time from home so she could spend more time with the children. They purchased a townhouse in Bethesda, Virginia. Things were settling down for them. They were becoming a real family. And now…

"Esther!" came John's voice from downstairs. "I'm making some omelet. Would you like some?"

No answer.

"Esther? Babe?"

She could hear his footstep coming up the stairs. This was not the way she would have wanted to tell him, but she couldn't wait.

John walked into the room and saw Esther kneeling on the bed, holding the Dreamcatcher Music Box he had given her. The Bloodwood Flute was in front of her. She had a curious grin on her face.

"What's going on?" he asked hesitantly.

"Come up here," Esther whispered.

"What…"

"Come here," she persisted.

John climbed onto the bed with her, careful not to bump her too much. When he was kneeling, facing Esther, she began.

"You remember when you gave me this?" she said, lifting up the beautiful Dreamcatcher Music Box.

"Yes. You made me the happiest man in the world that day."

"Did I?" she asked coyly.

"Of course!"

Esther began, unsure of how to proceed. "You said you loved our country, and that you loved me even more. You said that if I said 'yes,' you promised to protect me, to comfort me, to stand by me, and to support me. You promised to make me laugh every day, to apologize when you're wrong, to never take me for granted, and to tell me that you love me every day. Remember?"

"Yes. I remember." John said, taking Esther by the hands.

"Well, today is actually the day I will make you the happiest man on earth."

"What's special about today?" John asked.

Esther held the Dreamcatcher Music Box down to her abdomen and smiled, but John responded a confused look.

She rolled her eyes, smiling, and shook her head. "This Bloodwood Flute is my tie to my past; to my mother. This music box and these rings tie me to you, and to our future together."

She put the music box down and guided his hands to her womb. "And this… this is how I will make you the happiest man on earth!"

The next three seconds seemed like an eternity for John as he tried to figure out what Esther was telling him. Certainly, he was distracted by his own news… but then, like a lightning strike, he suddenly understood.

"What?! You're… We're… Are you sure?"

Esther nodded and John reached to grab her just as the smoke alarm went off.

"The omelet!"

Printed in the United States
by Baker & Taylor Publisher Services